The Dean Died
Over Winter Break

THE FIRST CHRONICLE OF BROTHER THOMAS

CHRISTOPHER LANSDOWN

THE DEAN DIED OVER WINTER BREAK
By Christopher Lansdown

Published by Silver Empire
https://silverempire.org/

Contents

This book is dedicated to my mother, who introduced me to murder mysteries, and to Ellis Peters, G.K. Chesterton, Dorothy L. Sayers, Agatha Christie, and Sir Arthur Conan Doyle, who gave the world the detectives I love so much.

Chapter 1

The first that Brother Thomas heard of the death of Jack Floden was in the office of his superior, Brother Wolfgang, in the morning of the twenty-ninth day of December in the year of Our Lord 2014. Brother Thomas had been a friar for seven years, two under permanent vows, in the Franciscan Brothers of Investigation. It was a small, and not very well known, order of consulting detectives.

That not all people are the same was a truth universally acknowledged until the social upheavals of the 1960s and 1970s. Within the Catholic Church in particular this was commonly expressed by the religious orders. They were formed not only for prayer but also for practical purposes, such as running schools and hospitals or providing security to travelers. The order to which Brother Thomas belonged, which was a Franciscan third order regular, was founded in France in 1823. It was formed to do the investigation required to assure bishops that in undertaking collaborations they were not joining themselves to criminal ventures. But the truth is a powerful thing and before long their scope widened as was the range of their geographical reach. In 1894 they were granted the status of a papal order and could go on their own authority outside of their native diocese.

In 1992, the order was asked to come to America, which it did, settling in the Bronx. Two brothers, one French and the other German, were selected to go: Brother Paul who was then 43, and Brother Wolfgang who was 39. By universal consent Brother Wolfgang was made the head of the house. Ordinarily within Franciscan third orders the head of a house is simply the person who takes care of paying bills and calling plumbers, but strange as it may sound to those who've only heard of Saint Francis but never tried to relate to him, Franciscans are intensely practical people. Since consulting detectives require someone to be in charge of meeting clients, vetting them, and deciding whether to take on cases, and since this skill set isn't far from what's needed to run a household, the head of the house was given these responsibilities too.

Brother Wolfgang was now 61. The twenty two years he had spent in America had filed off much of his accent. In his telling it had also given him the silver hair which he kept very neatly trimmed. He was of average height, or rather just slightly under it, and had light blue eyes, almost the color of ice beneath a blue sky. More than one person had been misled by his dignified bearing and careful politeness into missing that wide experience of the world which was visible in the intelligent movement of those blue eyes.

"You wanted to see me, Brother?"

"Yes," Brother Wolfgang replied. "I've just come back from a meeting with Archbishop Donovan."

Brother Thomas made no reply. His eyebrows might have raised very slightly.

"Please sit down," Brother Wolfgang said, gesturing to

the two chairs in front of his desk. Brother Thomas picked the less comfortable of the two and sat down on the edge of it, his eagerness well restrained, but still visible to the experienced eyes which looked at him.

"He has asked us to investigate a case which is unusual, even by our standards," Brother Wolfgang said, when Brother Thomas was as comfortable as he was going to make himself.

"Blackmail?" Brother Thomas asked, taking the clear invitation to guess.

"Murder."

Brother Thomas raised his eyebrows visibly even to an untrained eye this time.

"Murder! Am I correct in assuming that the murderer is unknown? There seems little reason to bring us in otherwise."

"You are indeed, correct."

Brother Wolfgang related the facts directly. On the morning of Monday the twenty second, Jack Floden, dean of the College of Liberal Arts & Sciences of Yalevard University, had been found dead in his office. His body was discovered face down on his desk, the window wide open and snow covering part of the floor. The dean had last been seen alive Friday afternoon, but with the body having been effectively refrigerated, the time of death could not be established. The school had closed early that day because of a snowstorm which started in the afternoon and lasted until Saturday night. What few meetings were scheduled had been canceled and almost nobody had been on campus until the storm let up.

"And that is, indirectly, why we have been consulted," said Brother Wolfgang.

"On its face, it *is* a difficult problem," Brother Thomas agreed.

"I was thinking, rather, of the fact that the universal lack of an alibi casts suspicion upon the entire faculty. Suspicion is a very destructive thing," said Brother Wolfgang.

"I imagine it might impact alumni donations," said Brother Thomas.

"It might. How the truth affects the guilty, we of course cannot help. But it is not right that suspicion should harm the innocent."

Brother Thomas nodded.

"Will you and Brother Francis investigate?"

An indecorous smile very nearly escaped onto Brother Thomas's lips.

"Certainly," he said.

Brother Wolfgang smiled. His long experience made it unnecessary to complement the younger man on hiding his enthusiasm. The inexperienced need people to know how clever they are. Brother Wolfgang was decades past needing explicit acknowledgement of what he already knew he was. Neither man thought that Brother Thomas was fooling anyone, and nor was he trying to.

"Excellent. Brother Paul and I will of course be available to you if you should need any assistance, though I doubt that you will."

Brother Thomas nodded.

"Who is it from the University who has called us in?" he asked.

"The president did. He has a friend who is a friend of the Bishop's."

"Did he say why he wants us?"

"The archbishop did not volunteer a reason, and I thought it impolite to ask what we don't need to know and will in any event find out."

"Will we need to have a pretext when we investigate?" Brother Thomas asked.

"I don't think so. You will of course need to discuss specifics with President Blendermore yourself before you go there, but I think that the public nature of murder means that this case will require less discretion than do most of our cases. The police will be publicly investigating, in any case. There is little to be gained by hiding the fact that one more investigation is going on as well."

They spoke for a few minutes about the particulars of how to get to Yalevard and where they would stay, then Brother Thomas left to find Brother Francis.

Brother Francis had been a friar only two years, and was still three years away from taking his permanent vows. He had no doubt he would take them when the opportunity finally came, but neither was he in a rush to take them. In the Franciscan Brothers of Investigation, a brother who has not yet taken permanent vows is partnered with a brother who has, and serves as an apprentice to him. Five to nine years is a lengthy apprenticeship, but consulting detection is a tricky business and there is no substitute for experience. Brother Francis was apprenticed to Brother Thomas, which was an unusual arrangement since Brother Thomas had been independent for only a few months before Brother Francis joined. Brother Wolfgang thought it best, and Brother Paul trusted him.

Brother Francis was in the library reading a book called, "Forty and Going Nowhere," which attempted to describe the psychology of the mid-life crisis. He looked up when he heard his name spoken.

"We just got a case."

"Judging by your face, it's an unusual one."

"Murder."

Brother Francis raised his eyebrows quite high.

"Wow," he said. "That is very unusual."

Brother Thomas nodded.

"I wonder that Wolfgang gave it to us," said Brother Francis.

"I think that the last time he or Paul investigated a murder was twenty years ago. And besides, he's too much of a realist not to know that I'd have stuck my nose in anyway."

"Your eye for detail might come in handy," Brother Francis mused, avoiding comment on Brother Thomas's self-deprecating remark.

Brother Thomas smiled.

"It often does, but who knows how much there will be left to observe after a forensics team has already examined the area. We can't expect them to have left it undisturbed for us."

"Speaking of which, I wonder how the police will take to us sticking our noses into their case?" Brother Francis mused.

"An excellent question, and while I can't see them welcoming us with open arms, I suspect that it will depend greatly on the person in charge."

The discussion lasted a few minutes more, mostly comprised of speculation and a few new questions questions without immediate answers. When the topic had been sufficiently discussed, Brother Thomas went to his room to call President Blendermore.

He returned several minutes later, looking on the whole like he had received good news.

"We're to stay at Dr. Blendermore's house—he has two guest bedrooms."

"What is his doctorate in?" Brother Francis asked.

Brother Thomas smiled at the way Brother Francis was certain he had looked up Dr. Blendermore's C.V. while talking to him on the phone.

"He has two, actually. The first is in philosophy. Ten years later he got one in economics."

Brother Francis nodded.

"Will we need a cover story?"

"Dr. Blendermore sees no need for one. That it would be nice if we didn't talk to the press, was the extent of his concern about what people would think of us being there."

"When do we leave?"

"I need to do laundry, and we should probably eat something before leaving. Amtrak has service to Yalevard but Brother Wolfgang said that we can take the Sentra since we might need to drive ourselves around once there. I would prefer to keep our options open, so we'll take the car. We might as well leave right after lunch."

Brother Thomas was known to have to wash his clothes three or even three four times because he would start the wash and then forget about them in the washer, until they'd spent so much time sitting damp that they needed to be re-washed. Brother Francis suspected that in this case Brother Thomas would manage it on the first try.

And indeed, they were packed and on their way to Yalevard by one o'clock.

Chapter 2

Yalevard was west and slightly north of Albany and the drive to it was as uneventful as a trip out of the New York metro area during the daytime could be. The brothers stopped only once and made good time; they arrived right as President Blendermore and his wife were sitting down to dinner. It was a hearty beef stew, of which there was plenty, in order to be prepared for guests without wasting food should they have come later. Stew can be left at a simmer for hours without being hurt, and is as good reheated as fresh.

Dr. Blendermore's first name, which he insisted on being called, was Ian. If he had Irish ancestry, it was not obvious; his light brown hair might have originated from anywhere in northern Europe. His face seemed to perpetually wear an inviting smile which didn't entirely hide the intelligence behind it. He was on the taller side of average, being perhaps five foot eleven, and he had a few becoming character lines in his face which suggested that he could still remember his fiftieth birthday party.

His wife's name was Staci. She was an elegant woman of approximately the same age as her husband, and though her face was smoother than his, it too had hints of a well exercised intelligence. In her case it was less hidden and in fact emphasized by her energetic manner. She had a darker coloring than he did, suggesting perhaps Spanish or Italian descent, with deep brown eyes and large curls in her shoulder length walnut-brown hair.

Their two children were both attending grad school at other universities and so weren't home for Christmas break.

"Are you associated with the university?" Brother Francis asked Staci as she set a bowl of stew in front of him.

"I teach biology," she said.

"Which made Dr. Floden your dean?"

She nodded.

"What sort of man was he?"

She sat down, drew in breath, and looked for words.

"That bad?" Brother Francis asked, smiling.

"No one wants to speak ill of the dead, but yes. Basically." Staci said. "He preceded me here, but from what I heard, he was a fairly popular man until he became dean. The power, such as it was, went to his head."

"How much power did he have?" asked Brother Thomas.

Ian cut in, as this was more in his domain.

"Professors are comparatively independent, though not absolutely so. They depend on students directly in so far as budgets are apportioned by enrollment and indirectly in so far as they like students. Deans have a fair amount of power over students, especially students who need something, or have fallen afoul of even trivial disciplinary rules. But even apart from that, all things are relative. You may have heard the saying that academic politics are extremely vicious because there's so little at stake? How important something is and how much people care about it are often unrelated. In

9

that sense, a dean might be very powerful indeed. Certainly, he has the power to create a great deal of resentment. If your next question is whether I know of anyone who Jack especially antagonized, I don't. There are some vestiges of the idea of the president of a university being the chief professor, and setting the example for the university, but largely my job is fundraising and community relations. I have less to do with the actual running of the university than probably is healthy."

"That's a pretty good picture of it," Staci said. "Jack's background was in biology, so he treated us decently, but he looked down, so I heard, on subjects like English and anthropology. I've even heard from a friend who's in theoretical physics that he didn't think the university should spend money or effort on their behalf. He was happy enough to take the university's cut of their research grants, though."

"That seems consistent," said Brother Francis.

In response to an inquiring look, he added, "If he thought the less practical disciplines were a drain on the university he would want to reverse that effect, as much as possible. Denying them money and taking their money both represent a reversal of the trend he thought reprehensible. Their doing research with outside funding was them wasting their own time and someone else's money."

"Consistent or not with his own principles, he was consistently mean to everyone but the practical scientists," Staci said.

"It's funny the things one learns," Ian said.

"You didn't talk about this before?" Brother Thomas asked.

"We worked at the same universities since before we were married, and we learned a long time ago that talking about academic politics can be a lot of fun at first, but makes us unhappy in the long run. So we try to talk about other, more cheerful things," Ian said.

"Telling Ian any of this would have just made his job harder," Staci said. "It's not like there's anything that he could have done about it. And it didn't really affect me, so it would have just been gossiping."

"We listen to a great deal of gossip, in our line of work," Brother Thomas said.

"Does much of it turn out to be reliable?" Ian asked.

"Most of it, we never find out. Where we do... probably about half and half. But the half that's false is often only partially wrong, and the half that's right is often misleading."

"That's gossip for you," Staci said.

"How are the police proceeding in the investigation?" Brother Thomas asked.

"Slowly," Ian said and sighed.

"To tell the truth, I don't really know. They haven't been forthcoming, or even particularly in touch. But I haven't heard of them focusing their attention on anyone, if that's what you're asking."

"Have they requested help from the state police?"

"Not that I've heard of."

"Is there anyone who would have known Dean Floden well?" Brother Francis asked.

"His secretary—Tiffany—couldn't help knowing him well, at least in his professional life. I'll make sure that Sonia—my secretary—introduces you to her tomorrow. I'm hoping that you won't take it amiss if I have her be the one to show you around and help you out. It's not that I'm too busy or are trying to keep my distance. Rather, she'll be a much better guide than I would be. Secretaries always know so much more about the internal working of an institution, since they do most of it."

"It's a cliche, but it's true," Staci added. "I think that Heinrich is the only one in biology who would do his paperwork without the department secretary's reminders and help. And he's German. From Germany, I mean. Elizabeth—the biology chair—would be completely lost without Mary Ann—our secretary."

"We will be most glad of her help," said Brother Thomas.

"Did Dean Floden have any hobbies?" Brother Francis asked.

"Not that he talked about," Ian said. "In college towns like this, usually everyone has some sort of hobby, but I can't remember him mentioning one."

"A lot of people are into walking," Staci added, "It's not much of a commitment, and there are tons of great trails around the campus and the university owns quite a lot of the surrounding land, and walking does have a positive image—if you walk you're doing something for your health, and everyone likes to look like they're taking care of themselves—it makes you look more responsible, and if anything does happen to you, you get more sympathy—but walking is very genteel—it's not like you sweat a lot, or need specialized equipment, though some people do use those things that look like ski poles."

"One more thing to ask his secretary," Brother Francis said, smiling.

"I had heard that the last the dean was seen was on Friday afternoon, on account of the weather. What was the storm like?" Brother Thomas asked.

"It was pretty bad, even by the standards of upstate New York," Ian said. "It had snowed the day before, and cleared up only late in the night. It began snowing again Friday morning, and was getting heavier by noon. It was supposed to turn into a full-on blizzard by five, so most buildings emptied out around two, I think. Since the students weren't around, we didn't bother with an official announcement."

"I don't think it was bad enough that we'd have closed early if it was finals week," Staci said.

"Probably not. The Friday before Christmas week is hardly the time to brave the winter like Vikings. At least, how I imagine Vikings would brave the winter. History was never my subject, but at least in popular culture they would never show fear before something as trivial as the weather."

"Given that they were primarily seafarers, I would think they were more practical than stupidly brave," Brother Thomas said. "There's a high minimum of courage necessary to be a sailor at all, but foolhardy sailors tend to die quickly. It is said that the Chinese respect lunatics, but the sea does not."

"Fair enough," Ian said. "Anyway, whatever the speculative-historic truth of whether Vikings would have closed their university in the same weather conditions, we unofficially closed ours."

He grinned, and the brothers and Staci laughed.

"Was the snow bad enough to prevent people traveling around during the blizzard such that Dean Floden would have had to have been killed either before or after it?" Brother Thomas asked.

"We only got about fourteen inches that night," Staci said. "That might stop someone who just got here from Texas, and certainly it would discourage walking for the fun of it, but for anyone who's been here at least one winter, it wouldn't prevent any important business. You'd walk, of course—cars are a pain in the neck on the hills around here, even sometimes with studded tires, and I don't think that anyone really uses studded tires on their cars any more. I mean, you can—it's legal, from some inconvenient date to some other inconvenient date—but I think everyone just uses snow tires. And in a blizzard you need one heck of a heater to keep the snow from binding up your wipers. It's not so bad if you're on the highway, since then the wind can make those new aerodynamic wipers push through it, but for driving around here, they're always going to get clogged with snow and ice. Besides, in a blizzard a car is much easier to recognize than a coat, scarf, and hat that you never use."

Brother Francis smiled at the shrewdness of this observation.

"It seems that we have a very wide-open field," said Brother Thomas.

"That's just the problem," Ian said. "It's at the heart of why I've asked you here. Scandal is of course bad for fund raising, which is unfortunately my main job, but more importantly, it's bad for community. Heaven knows that the community here is bad enough as it is with all of the bickering and in-fighting, to say nothing of the completely unreflective adherents of Modern Philosophy. Most of whom have barely heard of it and those who have, mostly didn't actually read it except to justify why they don't need to bother thinking. The English department is largely just fifth rate philosophers who are still here for a draft deferment because they haven't noticed that the Vietnam War has been over for forty years. The modern university is a mess, but even if it's largely abandoned the pursuit of truth out of the thirst for knowledge in favor of the pursuit of reputation out of the thirst for relevance, there is still real learning which goes on here too. One of the great principles of economics is that whatever can't go on forever, won't. And the modern university can't."

"Why not? The dark ages lasted for centuries." Brother Francis said.

"Because the modern dark ages aren't about barbarians winning through superior vitality. They're a binge fueled by the financial equivalent of an open bar and someone willing to get drinks for you so the bartenders can't tell how drunk you are."

"Do you mean the Pell Grants?" Brother Thomas asked.

"That's only part. Pell Grants let us charge far too much. That college is attended by affluent people leads people to conclude that college will make them rich. Universities offer credentials that are not subject to the disparate impact standard, so businesses outsource their discrimination to us—in effect, we sell them our ritual purity. Grad students and postdocs provide cheap labor that makes us cost less than in-house research for many businesses. The grad students and postdocs are willing to accept peanuts because they all hope to become tenured professors. None of that will last forever, and when the bubble bursts, universities are going to go through some very lean times. When that happens, the only people who won't leave are the people who are here for love.

"That's why we need to keep the university alive until that time comes. An unsolved murder would add an entirely new layer of problems. Academic politics are rancorous enough, but one can learn to navigate them. Outright mistrust and suspicion, I doubt *is* navigable. And scholars—real scholars—need a peaceful environment. Their desperation for peace—to be left alone to study their subject—is probably at least half of what got us into the modern mess. Cowardice is often successful in achieving peace, at least on a personal level. But that's beside the point. Scholars need peace, and if

15

the environment doesn't give them the peace they need, they will leave, and there will be nothing left but a four-to-six-year diploma mill for people who have mistaken correlation for causation."

"I can see why you are a university president. That sort of eloquence, if you can marry it to less candor, must bring a great deal of money into the endowment," Brother Thomas said.

"Pardon me. It's a subject near and dear to my heart, but I didn't mean to launch into a speech," Ian said.

Brother Thomas smiled, but not cynically.

"Please be assured that Brother Francis and I will investigate the case with all of our strength," he said.

Chapter 3

Miss Sonia Olivera turned out to be younger than Brother Thomas expected. He didn't have a specific idea of how old she was, but it was not common in his experience to hear a young person talked of as being competent. Yet she could be no more than twenty six or twenty seven. She was slightly tall with an athletic build, and wore her long, wavy black hair untied. Her face had a fierce beauty with evident traces of Arabic heritage, mixed with something that was harder to identify. Portuguese seemed plausible, given her family name. She wore a fashionable blazer, and might well have been dressing for the job she wanted, tempered with enough taste and humility not to make the practice offensive to her co-workers.

Ian had taken the brothers to his office in the morning and made the introduction, then turned them over to her care.

"Well, gentlemen, I am at your disposal. What would you like to see or who would you like to talk to?" she asked, as Ian left the room and went into his office.

"I should very much like to see the dean's office," Brother

Thomas said.

"That's Marduk Hall. Just let me get my coat."

She fetched it off of a coat rack not far away. It was a long, down-filled coat with a high collar but no hood. She threw a scarf and hat over her arm and led the way.

As they were walking down the stairs, she looked over her shoulder at Brother Thomas and said, "You're not going to observe that I grew up in a warm climate?"

"And that you played sports in high school and college, probably crew, took up rock climbing in grad school, which you still do though not as often, and that you run on a treadmill just to keep in shape and not because you're passionate about it? No, I'm not."

She looked a little startled. Then she smiled, arched her eyebrows and asked, "Why not?"

"I don't see the point in showing off by stating the obvious."

"Don't you?" she asked, though it was probably more of a statement than a question.

They had come to the front door, and she accordingly put on her fur-lined hat and wrapped her long scarf about her neck twice. Brother Francis zipped his winter coat over his habit, put a knit hat on, and thinking of the wind pulled his cowl up over the hat. Brother Thomas, who was wearing a thick woolen cloak, pulled its hood over his head then wrapped the left side over his right shoulder and the right side over his left shoulder, effectively doubling its thickness.

They didn't talk much, as it was overcast and windy. While it was not actually snowing, enough snow was being blown off of the roofs and branches that it might as well have been. It was not a long walk, except for the weather. Marduk Hall was less than two thousand feet away and the ground was reasonably level and the sidewalks mostly clear. They saw only one other person walking outside, by the look of him a professor bound to the post office to drop off a package.

Once they were inside and had shaken the snow off of their garments, Sonia said, "Okay, I'm guessing that you saw my running shoes, which are clean, in the clear bag, and that the rock climbing is because of the calluses on my fingers, but how did you know about crew?"

"It leaves a different callus pattern than rock climbing does. You've got the characteristic calluses at the base of the fingers and in the interior of the hand, but they're soft and intact, rather than recently worn. The ones on your fingers could be from either, of course. Would you like me to cold read your complicated relationship with your father? I also juggle, but I don't know any good card tricks."

"How do you know that my relationship with my father is complicated?"

"You're in your twenties. Of course your relationship with your parents is complicated. Besides, you're a woman. Your relationship with everyone is complicated."

Sonia smirked.

"So you know about women, do you?"

"I may not have sex with women but I was born of a woman, I have a sister I'm close to, and women do occasionally write things besides technical manuals for lawn mowers. Do you know whose offices these are?"

He gestured around.

Marduk Hall was not very big. It might have been a house at one time. There were four rooms on the bottom floor whose doors were closed, but they weren't labeled. There was also a bathroom and a closet.

"I believe that these are professors' offices, which are

used for visiting professors. Tiffany would know which. The dean's office is upstairs."

They went up the stairs which seemed to have been designed with Victorian ideas of how little room a staircase should have. They paused at the landing on the top floor.

"The carpenter who built these stairs was dedicated to his craft. Not one creak," Brother Thomas observed.

"I believe that office is occupied by a biology professor whose own office is being repaired, but I don't know for sure," Sonia said, pointing at the office on the back of the building. The next door was labeled Dean of the College of Liberal Arts & Sciences, and was closed.

"I assumed that you would want to look in here, so I got the key from Tiffany this morning. She's moved into the administration building temporarily."

Sonia produced the key, unlocked the door and pushed it open, then stood aside to let the brothers go in first. Brother Thomas inspected the railing closely, then took off his cloak and laid it over. Brother Francis tossed his coat onto one of the chairs on the landing next to the office door. Sonia unwrapped her scarf, but did not otherwise unbundle.

The dean's office consisted of two rooms which had evidently been partitioned off from a large master bedroom when the building was a house. The first room had several chairs and a table for waiting. There was also an office desk almost in front of the door to the larger office behind it.

"Tiffany has no family?" Brother Francis asked.

"Her parents are still alive, I think, but she's single and has no children, if that's what you mean."

"And Dean Floden?" Brother Thomas asked.

"Single. I think divorced... with one child? Maybe. I didn't talk with him often," Sonia said.

Brother Thomas got down on one knee and looked at the lock on the door to the inner room.

"Not forced, by the look of it," he said without surprise.

He stood up again and looked over the door. He walked inside without comment. Brother Francis looked at the knob and then at the door, then followed. Sonia looked at the knob and door when she thought that no one would see.

"How was he found?" asked Brother Thomas.

"On his desk," Sonia said.

"Did you see it yourself?" he asked.

"Yes. I got the news early, and came over here to... make sure Tiffany was okay. I got here a few minutes before the sheriff," she said.

"How was he sitting?"

Sonia took off her coat and tossed it over a chair, then sat down at the dean's desk with her arms folded, and her head laid on her arms.

"Like this," she said.

Brother Thomas studied her for a minute.

"Were the lamps and the furniture like they are now?" he asked.

Sonia got up from the chair and surveyed the desk. She looked extra hard at the lamp on the desk.

"Yes, but I don't think that this lamp used to be here. I mean, before that day. I can't be sure. It's not like I came here often," she said.

Brother Thomas looked around slowly.

"Were those pictures on the wall missing like they are now?" he asked.

"What pictures on the wall?" Sonia asked.

"The ones that aren't there," he said, pointing.

"I don't remember seeing any pictures there," she said.

Brother Thomas looked around the room again.

"Have the police released the cause of death?" he asked.

"Not that I know of," Sonia said.

"Was there blood?"

"Not that I saw."

"Would you have?"

"Yes," she said. "I came and looked around. Without touching anything."

"Of course," he said. "The window was open?"

"Yes, and snow had come in. An inch in the thickest part, I think, and it extended at least a foot into the room," she said.

He opened the window. It was of the sort normally found in houses. The sash moved easily considering the age of the building.

"How open was the window?"

"Fully," she said.

Brother Thomas noted that there was a storm window installed on the outside at some point, though there was no evidence for when it had been opened. Presumably at the same time as the window. He went to the window and looked out.

"What building is that?" he asked.

"That's the administration building."

"And that one over there?"

"Adler Auditorium."

"Used for special events?"

"Yes."

"Anything else?"

"Not typically."

He inspected the window casing, then walked over to the book shelves. He looked over them without saying a word for two and half minutes. He then walked over to the part of the room near the door. On the one side was a coat rack, and on the other an easy chair.

"Francis, what do you make of the book titles?" he said.

Brother Francis walked over to the bookshelf and looked over the books. Brother Thomas looked at the coat rack, which was bare.

"What was Dean Floden wearing, when he laid dead at his desk?" he asked.

Sonia closed her eyes for a moment.

"A button down shirt. I didn't notice his pants," she said.

"Can you remember details like whether he was wearing a tie?"

"I don't think so... There was more space between his collar and his neck than there would have been if he were wearing a tie."

"Why didn't you take pictures, by the way?"

"I didn't think Tiffany would approve, and she never left the room."

Brother Thomas got on his hands and knees and began to look around the easy chair.

"I would say that Dean Floden either chose his books because he thought he was an intellectual, or because he wanted to impress people sitting in his office. Since the most impressive sounding books are located closest to the chairs facing his desk, I would say it's the latter," Brother Francis said.

"You don't think that he read them?" Brother Thomas asked.

"His tastes would have been contradictory. Who outside of a philosophy department would read Nietzsche, Sir Thomas More, Darwin, and Kant?"

Brother Thomas let the question stand. He reached behind the easy chair and picked up something small. He stood up and looked at it in the light.

"The forensics team was not very thorough," he said.

"What is it?" Sonia asked.

"The cap to a syringe," he said.

He looked around the room, considering.

"And unless Dean Floden was an old fashioned diabetic, I suspect that we've found part of our murder weapon. Just to be on the safe side, I'll replace it as I found it."

He stood up and straightened his habit.

"Have I missed anything?" he asked.

"I don't think so," Brother Francis said.

"And what's your opinion, Dr. Olivera?" Brother Thomas asked.

"Okay, how did you know?" she asked.

"Your Facebook profile picture is of you and a friend in doctoral robes."

"You Facebook stalked me?"

"First, there is nothing analogous to stalking in looking at someone's public Facebook profile. Second, I didn't. I happened to see it when you checked Facebook on your computer, in your office."

"Looking over my shoulder while I use my computer seems worse."

"It is. Detection is not very compatible with respecting people's privacy. On the plus side, I won't tell anybody what I discover."

"And that makes it okay?"

"Close enough."

Sonia laughed, in spite of herself, and decided to accept that as an answer.

"I don't think you missed anything," she said.

Brother Thomas walked out of the room into the secretary's office. He paused, considering. He then examined the sides of the room, paying special attention to the floor underneath the furniture. His searching was rewarded with a second plastic cap, a duplicate of the first. He handed it to Brother Francis, who examined it, then handed it to Sonia.

"Another one? Does this mean he was a drug user, and this wasn't the murder weapon?" she asked.

"People who use needles by habit put the caps back on, to safely dispose of them," Brother Thomas said.

"It would also be very odd to inject himself in different places, and especially someplace relatively public when someplace more private was ten feet away," Brother Francis said.

"It could be Tiffany's. She might use her own office normally, and have to retreat into the dean's office on occasion," Sonia said.

"Does she strike you as someone so dedicated to her drug habit that she shoots up at work?" Brother Thomas asked.

"Well, no," Sonia said.

"All things are possible, but not all things are probable," Brother Thomas said, and smiled.

"But the improbable does happen," Sonia said.

"All too often. Reality, unlike fiction, doesn't have to be believable, and all that. You are right that when we make deductions, we risk being wrong. But we must, for if we refuse to make deductions, we guarantee that we will be wrong."

"There's a difference between being ignorant and being wrong," she said.

"Yes, though it would be a more practical distinction if one could step outside of time and not have to make any decisions. Until you figure out how to do that, you will do things, and whether they're out of ignorance or out of error, there is little difference compared to making decisions based on the truth. If we make deductions and act on them, we might prove or disprove them. If we refuse to conclude anything out of the fear of concluding incorrectly, we'll never know anything at all."

He took the cap from her and put it back where he had found it. He stood up and looked around. There were several filing cabinets against the wall opposite to the chairs, so he opened them and glanced through their contents.

"Universities seem to run on a great deal of paperwork," he said.

"Trees and trees worth," Sonia agreed.

He walked to Tiffany's desk, sat down, and tried the drawers.

"They're locked," he said.

"This is a dean's office. There could be confidential or important stuff in her drawers," Sonia said.

"But not in the filing cabinets?" he asked.

He inspected the lock, then reached inside of his habit and brought out a homemade lockpicking kit.

"If you dislike the invasion of people's privacy, I suggest that you avert your eyes," he said.

Sonia came closer to get a better view. The lock was a very simple one, and he opened it after only thirty seconds of work. The drawer above the space for the chair contained the standard assortment of pens, pencils, paper clips, rubber bands, and other stationery supplies.

The top side drawer contained an assortment of larger stationery items like a stapler, a hole punch, a box of assorted binder clips, and other things no one would ever lock up. It was the bottom side drawer that contained something that might justify a lock: a large box of condoms.

"Now we know why she locked the desk before leaving,"

he said.

"Her boss?" Brother Francis asked.

"We don't have conclusive evidence, since the waste baskets are lined with disposable plastic liners, and are currently empty. Still, yes," Brother Thomas said.

"She has condoms in her desk so she must be banging her boss?" Sonia asked, incredulously. "People have condoms for all sorts of reasons. Lots of women have sex on dates, and want to make sure that protection is available. I get why you wouldn't know that, but this is a great example of why it's so dangerous to jump to conclusions."

"My dear girl, I do not have sex myself, but I know far more about it than you do or, most likely, ever will. Do you have any idea what nine out of ten of our cases are?" Brother Thomas asked.

"I don't know... finding out what sins people committed?" she said.

"What?" he said, taking his turn to be incredulous. He looked at Brother Francis as if to ask if he could believe such a thing was just said. He looked back at Sonia.

"Is that supposed to be related to confession?" he asked, trying to make sense of what he just heard.

"I suppose," she said. "I'm not Catholic. I don't really know what you do."

"Obviously," he said. "First, confession is something you do when you feel sorry for your sins, that is, for the things you did wrong. No one makes you go, and nothing happens to you if you don't, except that you feel bad."

"Why would you feel bad?" Sonia asked.

"For the same reason that your head hurts if you have a headache and don't take aspirin. And confessions are confidential. We've never investigated anything related to what somebody said in confession. If a priest were to ask us to investigate something related to a confession, he'd have his priestly faculties revoked."

"I think I meant more finding out what they didn't say in confession," Sonia said.

"Why would we care?" Brother Thomas asked.

"Well, for the reason priests hear confessions?" Sonia said.

"Priests hear confessions to help people get rid of their sins. I don't care what any other man's sins are; that's between him and God. No. Most of our cases are suspected marital infidelity. A husband or a wife is worried that their wife or husband is cheating on them, and comes to us for help. They're right about a third of the time. In the last seven years, I've learned a great deal about how people hide sex and where they keep their condoms."

"You're a very strange monk," she said.

"I'm not a monk," he said. "I'm a friar. Monks are supposed to build enclaves which protect those inside from the evil of the world, so that people can find rest. They build fortresses, and man the walls, and invite the world in to take refuge from the world. Friars are supposed to go out into the world and serve people wherever we find them. They're two very different, though complementary, disciplines."

"I'm sorry for getting that wrong, but what difference does that make to how much you're supposed to know about sex?" Sonia asked.

"Monks might possibly be innocent, in the sense of ignorant, of the world's evils. Even there, I suspect that if they were, they'd still be a lot less ignorant than *you* would think. But it would at least be possible and consistent with their mission. It wouldn't make any sense for a friar to be ignorant of the evils of the world. We're supposed to be innocent only in the other sense of the word. We're supposed to know the sins of the world, but only theoretically—not from experience. And yes, that can be dangerous if you're not cut out for it. That's why you have to make temporary vows for five years before you can make permanent vows."

If Brother Thomas had grown horns, Sonia would not have looked at him very differently than she did then.

Brother Thomas sighed, and said, not unkindly, "It's a big world, and there are many different kinds of people in it. The word 'catholic' means 'universal', and the Catholic Church is universal not in the sense of being a cookie cutter that can make everyone the same, but in the sense of being able to find a place for every kind of person. Few people are made to be friars, and few friars are made to be detectives. In that sense, I *am* very strange, as are my brothers in the order—that's why there are so few of us. You will probably never be able to make sense of us according to your experience."

Sonia considered this for a minute, then set it aside.

"So what does it mean that Tiffany was sleeping with her boss?" she asked.

"Possibly nothing. Most things that we find out end up meaning nothing," Brother Thomas said.

"It does make Tiffany a suspect. If the dean cheated on her, it would be a motive for murder," Brother Francis said.

"Bear in mind that it's early days yet. That someone is a suspect does not mean much at this stage," Brother Thomas said.

"So what next?" Sonia asked.

Brother Thomas looked around.

"I want to take a closer look at the other offices. Do you know who would have the keys to them?" he said.

"Do you mean other than the professors using them right

now?" Sonia said.

"Yes."

"There's somebody in Administration who has keys for all of the doors on campus, and the cleaning staff would have keys for the rooms they're supposed to clean," she said.

Brother Thomas nodded, and tried the other door on the landing. It was locked. He went downstairs and tried the three offices on the ground floor. They were all locked.

He opened the door to the bathroom. It was a single occupant bathroom, though it did have a privacy door in front of the toilet. The style looked like it had been accreted over the decades. Possibly it had been converted from something smaller to something more spacious. Brother Thomas opened the door to the toilet and looked at it.

"This is interesting," he said.

Brother Francis and Sonia followed him in. Plainly visible on the toilet seat were two dirt smudges, one on each side.

"Someone was messy?" Sonia said, dubiously.

"Someone came in, went straight to the bathroom, or at least didn't go far before coming here, and stood on the toilet seat. You can somewhat make out the footprints on the floor, though they're quite smudged. We must find out when the bathroom was last cleaned," Brother Thomas said.

He checked the time on his cell phone.

"I think we're done here, for the moment, at least. I would like next to talk with Tiffany, but we need to head to church now in order to make it to daily mass. You're welcome to come, but we can find our own way there and meet you at your office afterward."

"I'm not Catholic, remember?" Sonia said.

"Do you think that I forgot?" Brother Thomas replied.

"Are you trying to convert me?" she asked.

"Not at all. I didn't think you would want to come, but I did not wish to be unwelcoming. Daily mass rarely lasts longer than about thirty five minutes, so we should see you in a little over an hour."

"I'm coming," she said.

Whether she did it merely for the pleasure of seeing Brother Thomas surprised, or just to be contrary, or for some other reason, even she wasn't certain. But certainly surprise was a consideration and she was not disappointed. He had been turning to leave, and checked sharply when she said that. He looked at her, as if trying to peer into her soul, then visibly gave it up and said, simply, "As you wish."

They went upstairs to get their coats, then walked silently to the church.

Chapter 4

The brothers and Sonia left the church with an inconsequential solemnity. Sonia because she had, to some degree, invaded what clearly mattered a great deal to her two companions. She hadn't expected them to take it so seriously. An intense and intelligent person herself, she had never before experienced other intense, intelligent people treating as profoundly serious something which ordinary people also took seriously. She didn't consciously think of herself as part of an elite which lived a different life from the unwashed masses. Those without any experience of those who do consciously think of themselves as above the unwashed masses might think that doing so unconsciously can be worse.

Brother Thomas was solemn as he walked simply because his mind was elsewhere: he was contemplating how to approach their upcoming interview with Dean Floden's secretary. Brother Francis was solemn because he was thinking about the readings of the day and how its theme might be worked into an article for a magazine to which he sometimes contributed. He wasn't ignoring the case, he simply had the ability to suspend thinking about things until he had enough facts that he might come to a conclusion. Brother Thomas, by contrast, had a prodigious memory and the ability to formulate a dozen alternative theories—each contingent on the results of future investigations—without getting attached to any of them.

It was Brother Thomas who spoke first.

"How well do you know Tiffany?"

"Not very well. Mostly we'd talk on the phone when one of us was calling the other about some official business. She's a co-worker. I wouldn't call her a friend."

"You won't mind introducing us, then?"

"Not at all."

They walked on in silence until they came to the administration building. There they found that Tiffany was given a small private office whose normal occupant was on vacation. She was somewhere in her mid-thirties, with straight, shoulder length brown hair carefully arranged and just a touch of skillfully applied makeup. Her clothes were less ambitious than Sonia's but showed more style born of longer experience.

"Hi Tiffany," Sonia said. "This is Brother Thomas and Brother Francis. Ian asked them to come and look into Jack's death with an eye toward protecting the interests of the university."

"Nice to meet you," Tiffany said to the brothers, without enthusiasm.

"First, you have our condolences," said Brother Thomas.

"Thank you."

"It must have been quite a shock."

"It was."

"Was it you who found him?"

She nodded.

"What did you think when you saw him?"

"That he was asleep."

"With the window open?"

"That did seem strange."

If she was trying to cut the interview short by being un-responsive, she was using the wrong tactic. Brother Thomas especially distrusted people who made conversations feel like tooth-pulling.

"What did you do?"

She sighed. It was too open-ended a question to avoid.

"I called out his name."

Brother Thomas waited without changing his expression in the slightest. The silence lasted only about five seconds, but it seemed longer.

"He didn't answer so I went in and touched his shoulder."

"It felt wrong?"

"Yes."

"Cold?"

"Yes."

"Rough?"

"I guess."

Brother Thomas considered her for a moment, weighing probabilities as to why she would be so unhelpful. Tiffany was looking down at her desk and didn't see his expression grow a few shades more intense.

"I don't care that you don't want to talk with me, and I'm reasonably confident that you didn't murder the dean. Clear-ly your relationship with him was purely sexual, or rather, your sexual relationship was purely about achieving power over him, since his death is just an inconvenience to you. The thing I don't know is whether you might have seen anything which might be helpful in figuring out who *did* murder the dean. I won't appeal to your university spirit, since obviously this is just a job to you, but has it occurred to you that whoever did murder Dean Floden has made your job a great deal harder? Especially if the nature of your relationship with him became public?"

"Are you threatening me?"

"No. It's not my job to make confidential matters public. That's what we have the police for. With their powers to search everything and read emails and confiscate your phone, they tend to find things out. I'm not threatening you. I'm pointing out that I'm the lesser of two evils."

"You are a cynical bastard," she said, not entirely disapprovingly.

"The world has more than justified it," he said.

"And yet you're a monk?"

"Do you think I became a monk because I have a high regard for the relations between the sexes?"

She eyed him with a grudging respect.

"If I help you, do you think you can solve this quickly? You're right that I'm not fond of the police. The sheriff is more than usually thick for a man, and not at all polite."

"God accomplishes all things according to the intentions of His will. The rest of us merely try and mostly fail. That being said, that is my plan."

"That's about the best I'm going to get, isn't it?"

"If you can find a better offer, please let me know—I might be interested in it too."

She smiled.

"I will. So what do you want to know?"

"What was the dean wearing when you got in? A coat?"

"Just a shirt."

"Was it the same shirt he was wearing during the last day you saw him alive?"

She thought for a moment.

"No. It was a white shirt and he wore a blue shirt last Friday."

"Is there a record of who Dean Floden met on that Friday?"

"He didn't have any appointments that day."

She smirked as she said it.

"Do you remember who stopped in?"

The smirk turned into a smile.

"Five people stopped in. Dr. Buskirk, Dr. Cassidy, Dr. Marten, Jordan Blakely, and Dr. Darrel. In that order. He had screaming matches with Dr. Buskirk and Dr. Marten. Shakira—Dr. Cassidy—dropped in just to hand in some forms. Jordan is a foreign student who sold Jack weed. I guess I should say supplied. And I don't think that Dr. Darrel actually saw Jack. I saw him coming down the stairs as I was coming in from lunch, and Jack had left for lunch before me and got back afterwards because the provost called him and asked him to come to her office."

"Do you know what about?"

"Jack didn't want to say, so I'm guessing that it was another sexual harassment complaint against him."

"He had them before?"

"Twice in the last five years."

"Do any of the Dean's enemies stand out in your mind as likely to have been the one to end him?"

"To tell the truth, not really. He was a bastard, but he was smart enough to keep on decent terms with most people, at least to work with them. Among his equals, at least. He pissed off enough professors, I suppose, but he tended to be pretty equal opportunity. I can't think of anyone who was more screwed over than anyone else. I mean, within a department. He did hate the liberal arts and the soft sciences."

"Do you know what the fights with Dr. Buskirk and Dr. Marten were about?"

"Dr. Buskirk lost a grant which was conditional on the university taking less of it than normal, and he blamed Jack."

"Would that have been under Dean Floden's discretion?"

"No, but he wanted Jack to try to convince the provost, and Jack refused. In fact, Jack actually did his best to convince the provost not to give in."

"And the fight with Dr. Marten?"

"Money and respect. She wanted more of both. He gave her less of the second. A lot less."

"I imagine he was on good terms with his marijuana dealer?"

"He didn't have money problems, if that's what you mean."

"Do you know if he had any other sexual partners?"

"We didn't talk about it, but there's one student I've had my suspicions about. She's a grad student in the biology department. Pretty, if you're into skinny blonde bitches. Not real well endowed, but she makes the most of what she's got, if you know what I mean."

"I can guess. Was Dean Floden easily fooled?"

"When a hot twenty-one-year-old is interested in an unhappy fifty six year old man, she could be flat and he wouldn't care."

"What's her name?"

"Audrey... I forget her last name. I think it starts with an 'F'. If you give me your phone number, I'll text you when I remember."

Brother Thomas took one of his business cards out of his pocket and gave it to her.

"The Franciscan Brothers of Investigation. 'The Truth will set you free,'" she read. "Is that from Shakespeare?"

"By modern standards, you're quite close. It's from the Bible."

"I'm surprised I recognize it, then," she said with a mischievous smile.

"So am I," he said, without guile. "One final question: which of you left the office first?"

"I did. I left around 2:30."

"Thank you. When you remember that name, and if you come across anything else that might help us to wrap this investigation up quickly, please text me."

Tiffany nodded, and they left.

Chapter 5

When they got outside the administration building, Sonia blurted out, "I cannot believe her. I can't believe you were right that she *was* sleeping with Jack! And I can't believe how... cold she is. I mean, she doesn't care at all that he's dead. And I can't believe how well you got along with her!"

"It's my job to get along with people," Brother Thomas said.

"Did you really become a friar because you think that men and women can't get along?"

"I never said that I did."

"You implied it."

"I didn't. I implied that I was well aware of the cynical view of the situation. And I am. That doesn't mean that I believe it to be the most accurate view, though in fairness you have to admit that the screamingly high divorce rate—together with the fact that the only reason it isn't higher is that so many people aren't even bothering to get married—certainly is a point in favor of that view."

"Just because people do it wrong doesn't mean that it can't

be done right. And lots of people do do it right," she said.

He smiled.

"Abusus non tollit usum. You're quite correct that if things are done badly, so much the worse for the world but it doesn't harm the ideal. However, to someone who thinks that she's isolated because she alone sees through the fairy tales which people tell themselves for comfort, it would not have been helpful to point that out."

"So the ends justify the means?" Sonia demanded.

"That is a much abused phrase. Of course I don't endorse doing something intrinsically evil because one of its side effects is desired, but please tell me: other than the ends, what could possibly justify the means?"

"What do you mean?" she asked.

"There's no such thing as an intrinsically good means. Sawing a board could be part of building somebody a house or building a gallows to lynch him on. Piercing somebody with a sharp piece of metal could be part of murdering him or part of cutting a tumor out of him."

"That's a bit technical for me," she said.

"In this particular case, there's nothing inherently truthful or deceitful in telling somebody that you understand their point of view. I put things very differently when I was talking with Tiffany than I would with you because I was talking with her and not with you. That doesn't mean that I was honest with one of you and not the other. Human language is nothing but a collection of conventions by which we attempt—and largely fail—to communicate ideas. There's no way of saying anything that is natural to *me*—if I were alone on a desert island, I wouldn't talk at all. If a man is going to open his mouth, it's his job to pick his words according to what will be best understood by the person he's talking to.

That's what I did."

Sonia considered that for a moment.

"I think it's scary that you're so good at being understandable to her," she said.

"Do you know why we investigate marital infidelity?" he asked.

Sonia didn't see what that could have to do with what they were talking about, but she took a stab anyway.

"Because that's the most common thing people need investigated, and you have to live?"

Brother Thomas shook his head.

"We don't make money from our investigations. We're supported by our host diocese. While occasionally people who we've helped will give us money in gratitude, that's not part of our operating budget."

"Why, then?"

"Because when we investigate infidelity, we investigate it thoroughly. We find out, as much as possible, not just what happened, but why it happened. And then we do our best to help fix that and get the couple to reconcile. We do what we do in order to repair lives.

"Priests, because they hear confessions and forgive sins and give counsel, are often called doctors of souls. You might call us the specialist surgeons of souls. We find the hidden problems, that people won't speak about and couldn't even if they would. We delve into the worst that human beings do—into the things that even they can't explain—in order to find the person buried underneath the sin. Then we do our best to bring them back up with us. We see some of the harshest ugliness there is. Do you know why a person would cheat on their loving spouse with the full knowledge that it will wreck their children's lives when the family falls apart? Do you know why a man would turn his own children against their mother so that they refuse to talk to her? Do you know why a woman would torture her children without leaving a mark, and scare them into not telling anyone? Do you know why people fake crimes and get their spouse arrested and sent to prison?"

He stared at her expecting an answer, with an intensity that was almost frightening. She tried to voice an answer or two, but in the face of that earnest inquiry, they died unspoken. Easy answers and joking evasions wouldn't do. She shook her head in the negative.

"I do," he said. "I've seen every one of those at least twice. And do you know what it's taught me?"

"What?" she asked, faintly. Sonia felt like she was talking with a monster. She was almost afraid of what lessons it had learned from the worst that human beings had to offer.

"That the love of God is greater than all human evil. That where sin abounds, grace abounds more. I've seen some of the worst there is, and it doesn't prove that life is meaningless. It proves that life is worth living. And it proves that we need God. I'm probably the most cynical person you've ever met, or ever will meet. But that doesn't mean that I think life is bad. It means I know how much evil can exist in a good world. That's what the faith gives me: I can stare evil in the face without blinking, because I know that it's not the whole story."

He took a deep breath, then continued, a little more relaxed.

"I'm sure that's scary, if you're used to blinking. I don't know what to tell you, except that closing your eyes is not the way to be happy. If there's something that you're not supposed to look at, then look at it. If there's something you're not supposed to think about, then think about it. If something is too horrible to face, face it. Because the truth *will* set you free."

"You scare me," she said, but it was an observation, neither a criticism nor a request to stop.

He shrugged his shoulders.

"Comfort is overrated," he said.

They stood there in silence for a few moments.

"Who would have the authority to read Dean Floden's email?" he asked.

"The provost, I think," she said.

"Then we have two things to talk with her about."

"Before we do, there is something that bothers me," said Brother Francis.

"What's that?" asked Brother Thomas.

"The dean's secretary said that Dean Floden was usually careful not to push people too far. Yet the manner of his death, if we are correct that he was injected with poison, seems both personal and deliberate. You don't fill a syringe and inject it into a person in the heat of the moment. And you can't do it from a distance. You have to get very close and overpower a person, to inject him with something against his will. How did someone get to this point, if Floden was careful not to cross the line?"

Brother Thomas thought about it for a few seconds.

"The obvious explanation would be that he slipped up and crossed the line," he said.

"But someone who is careful doesn't toe the line. According to his secretary, he was careful to keep from being outright offensive. She didn't say that he normally stopped short of driving people into homicidal rages. From the sound of it, Floden was manipulative. Manipulative people have at least an instinctive sense of how far you can push people. They don't usually blunder into fighting words."

"Logically, if the motive for his death was not something he could have prevented—on the assumption that if it was, then he would have—it must have been something he couldn't have prevented," Brother Thomas said. "If he had any money, perhaps he was killed by an heir? If not, perhaps someone who wanted his job? It seems far-fetched, but I suppose he could have been a witness to a crime. We do know at least that he was a witness to the possession of marijuana with intent to distribute."

"There are intermediates. Someone who decided that the world would be better off without Floden, and did it for the sake of the world," Brother Francis said.

"You mean like someone defending a loved one from blackmail?"

"We have no reason to suppose it was blackmail, but something like that would fit."

"That's something to keep an eye out for, to be sure," Brother Thomas said.

They proceeded to the provost's office. Conveniently, she was in.

"Hello, Sonia," she said, as they walked in to her office. The provost was a an older woman, with more than a few wrinkles in her face. Her silver hair might have been a ploy to gain respect if her energetic manner and natural confidence didn't make it clear that she needed no help in that direction. She wasn't tall, and was thin but moved in a way that suggested she worked out regularly and would probably live to be one hundred. Her clothes matched the dignity of her office.

"Hi Martha," Sonia said as she walked in. She waited until the brothers were in the office and in a convenient place for introductions. "This is Brother Thomas and Brother Francis. They're detectives. Ian has asked them to look into Jack's death. To see if they can help the police bring the investigation to a quicker close."

The Provost looked a little surprised as she surveyed the two robed figures standing before her. It didn't last, though. In a moment her long practice at taking in news without showing emotion brought a cautious smile to her lips.

"Welcome, gentlemen. Please, sit down."

She gestured at the chairs in front of her desk, then sat down herself.

"Obviously murder is bad at any time and in any place but this is an especially unpleasant problem for us. What can I do to help?"

This self-mastery did not escape Brother Thomas and he judged it would be best received to get straight to the point.

"The first and most obvious question would be: what do you think were the top four motives for killing Dean Floden?" Brother Thomas said.

"You mean other than for just being a bastard?"

"Yes."

"That's a good question. I assume you mean among the faculty, since the students weren't here when he was killed?"

"Some of the grad students are still present, I understand."

"True. Well, he did generally make himself unpleasant to everyone but those in the practical sciences. For the most part it wouldn't bother tenured professors in the disciplines he didn't like, but he certainly made life hard on those departments when they wanted to put somebody up for tenure.

He would complain about their grade distributions being too high. Which often wasn't false, mind you, but it was still a pretext. Tenure is a very precious thing, and to not get tenure at the end of a tenure track position can be very damaging to a career. I don't recall anyone getting denied tenure this semester, but that's one place to look. And when you get down to it, departments don't like it when one of theirs is denied tenure. I've never heard of anyone killing over it before, but there's always a first time for everything.

"He would tend to make himself unpleasant over shared space allocation, but most departments have jurisdiction over their own buildings, so his power was limited in that regard.

"There have been a few students, over the years, for whom Jack didn't exercise any mercy that would have been within his discretion. And again, that tended to be applied very unequally. He might let biology students off with a reprimand and expel a psychology major or an English major for the same offence. People can take it very hard when favorite students are expelled."

"There are also, we have heard, some cases of misconduct by the dean which could cause people to seek revenge," Brother Thomas said.

"Ah. You've heard about that? Well, I should have mentioned it. I've received complaints about Jack three times, the most recent being Friday morning. That is, the morning of the last day he was seen alive. The previous times were quite some time ago, and those students haven't been here for years."

"How were those cases resolved?" Brother Thomas asked.

"There was insufficient evidence to do anything. To be honest, the first two seemed like cases of consensual relationships which ended badly. Jack can be charming when he wants to be—*could* be charming when he want*ed* to be, I mean—and people can—could take offense when he turned that off. But ceasing to flirt with someone is not a punishable offense."

She shrugged her shoulders.

"Either way, there wasn't enough evidence to force our hand and we weren't going to cause a scandal if we could avoid it."

Brother Thomas nodded.

"What about the most recent one?"

"That one was different. He got a bit careless this time. Or perhaps he was just optimistic. Either way, he was flirting with someone who didn't want to be flirted with, and if she was telling the truth, he pushed past plausible deniability. Which would be odd for him, but then even careful people are sometimes careless. It's moot now, of course, but I don't know what it would have come to. My guess is that the girl would have been willing to settle quietly, as long as she didn't think that he was getting off the hook entirely.

"I actually met with Jack that afternoon about it. He reacted as you might expect. He didn't deny the facts of the case, but didn't think it mattered. He figured that she could be bought off or placated easily enough, and that it wouldn't really affect him."

"Did he explain why he had been careless?" Brother Francis asked.

"Jack never offered explanations and I was too angry with him for jeopardizing the university's reputation to ask," Martha said.

"From what you said a moment ago, though, you thought that Dean Floden was right. I mean, that the girl could be placated cheaply enough, and thus it wouldn't really affect him much," Francis said.

"Whether it wouldn't affect the *university* much isn't the same thing as whether it wouldn't have affected *Jack* much," she said, in a tone which gave the words ominous significance.

"Tell me: who do you think would be the worst person for the murderer to turn out to be? From the university's perspective, I mean?" Brother Thomas asked.

The provost evidently took no offense at the question. She thought about it for only a moment before answering.

"Probably a senior member of the administration—another dean, me, or the president. Anyone on the faculty would be pretty bad, really. A student wouldn't be much better, unless it were something really random like being mentally ill. If it was a member of the staff, like the cleaning person, it wouldn't be so terrible, but on the other hand it would show that we don't screen our people well. There really isn't a good option, at this point. Well... it wouldn't be so bad if it was revenge for something that happened a long time ago, before he came to the university. Like if he witnessed some crime and his testimony sent the perpetrator to prison for twenty years, and he just got out last month."

"It seems unlikely, but nothing in this world is certain," Brother Thomas said.

He thought for a moment, considering other questions, then shifted subjects.

"On a practical note, it would be very helpful if we could look through Dean Floden's email. It's my understanding that you would have the authority to give us permission," he said.

"Certainly," she said. "Technically his email is his property, but we have the right to read it for security purposes, for which I have no problem deputizing you. If not in the course of investigating his murder, then you can help investigate the allegations against him. Even with him dead, the university is still on the hook for his behavior."

She picked up her phone.

"Incidentally, if you find out anything which might help me in that regard, you will pass it on, won't you?"

"We live to serve," Brother Thomas said.

She smiled, not entirely sincerely, then found the number for computer services, on the directory taped to her wall, and dialed it.

"Hello, this is the provost. May I speak with Steven, please?"

She waited a moment, but not long.

"Hello Steven. I've got something unusual for you. There are two monks here who are investigating an issue for us relating to Dean Floden. They will need access to his email. Hm. I think it's best if they come to you and you show them; this way we're not making any copies. I don't know whether he has any family who would object, but it's better to stay on the safe side. Their names are Brother Thomas and Brother Francis. They'll be the ones in the brown robes with white ropes tied around their wastes: you can't miss them. Thank you."

She hung up the phone and looked up. Brother Thomas rose.

"Thank you for your time. If anything more comes to your attention, please let us know."

"Thank you for looking into this, and I will," she said.

As they walked out the door, he stopped, turned, and asked, "Oh, one more thing. When did the dean leave your office?"

"He wasn't here that long. Perhaps half an hour? I sent a few emails after he left. I'll check my sent folder and see when I sent them."

She sat down at her desk and navigated quickly through her email until she found what she was looking for. Though not generally adept at using computers, she spent so much time reading and sending email that she couldn't help but know her away around the email program.

"I stopped sending email at 12:55, and started sending them again at 1:38. Figure a few minutes on either side of that, but that's pretty close," she said.

"Thank you," Brother Thomas said.

When they got outside, Sonia sighed.

"I'm learning a lot of things about this university that I never wanted to know."

"This is a difficult job if you don't love the things you investigate," Brother Thomas said.

"Aren't the things you love the things you don't want to learn bad things about?" she said.

"No. Of course you wish that there was nothing bad to find out, but the things you love are the things you can stand to learn evil of. The things you don't love must be good or you'll hate them. The things you love, you can love despite their flaws."

"That might be. I suppose that I love the ideal of the university more than the real university," Sonia said.

"That's common," he said.

"It would be nice if the real university were closer to the ideal," she said.

"It would indeed. On a more practical subject, it's time for lunch. What would you recommend? We'll eat just about anything."

"The best places to get food are an Indian restaurant, a Chinese restaurant, a pizza place, and a diner," she said.

"I'm quite fond of Chinese food," Brother Thomas said.

"I could go for any of them," Brother Francis said.

"I like Chinese too, so let's go there," Sonia said.

She led the way down the hill towards Main Street, where most of the restaurants were located.

"So where do you see the investigation going next?" Sonia asked as they walked.

"There are several people who saw Dean Floden on the last day that he was seen alive whom we have not yet talked to. I would like to speak with them, though I'm not sure if that's a task for today," Brother Thomas said.

"What about speaking with the police?" Brother Francis asked.

"If the police will talk with us, it would be very convenient to learn what they know. They have some very useful powers that enable them to learn quite a lot. I'm not sure that the sort of things they're good at learning are a place for us to start, however."

"What do you think of the idea the murderer is a recently released criminal?" Sonia asked, smiling.

"It doesn't seem likely, but unlikely things are still worth looking into. For example, we should try to look into Dean Floden's financial situation. Is there anyone who might have been in town who would have benefited from his death? It would also be interesting to find out how the next dean will be selected."

"Someone might have killed him to open up his job?" Sonia asked.

"Do you have any evidence to rule out the possibility?" Brother Thomas asked.

Sonia treated it like a rhetorical question, so Brother Thomas continued.

"There is of course the possibility of someone Floden wronged here on campus taking their revenge. We'll need to talk with Tiffany again once we have a list of specific questions to ask her, which I have no doubt will develop in the next day or so. I would be curious to know what sort of girl this Audrey is, and whether Floden did in fact have a sexual relationship with her."

"That would give Tiffany a motive, wouldn't it? I mean, jealousy has led people to murder before," Sonia said.

"True, though she didn't strike me as being attached to Floden," he said.

"Jealousy can come from wounded pride and vanity, as often as from disappointed affection," Brother Francis said. "Still, I'm inclined to agree with you. If she had killed him, I think she would have done it further away from herself. In the office they both worked in... seems too close to home."

"We won't rule her out, but we'll put her on the back burner for now," Brother Thomas said.

They arrived at the restaurant, and the conversation shifted to subjects more suitable for public discussion. It was carried on primarily by Sonia and Brother Francis. Though polite, Brother Thomas was withdrawn. Sonia guessed, correctly, that he was preoccupied with the case. He would answer questions without unreasonable brevity, but there was no subject which would draw him out.

Brother Francis ate heartily, and seemed to enjoy himself, while Brother Thomas did only a little bit more than peck at his food. Perhaps that was why he was so thin.

After they paid (they requested separate checks), the discussion turned back to the case.

"Where to now?" Sonia asked.

"Before we talk to more people, I would like to look through Dean Floden's email. As that is likely to take more than a few hours, and since we've already kept you from your work all morning, perhaps we should split up here. Brother Francis and I can find our way to the computer services building, and the provost has already introduced us, so you need not be bothered with us for the time being," Brother Thomas said.

Sonia looked surprised.

"I don't mind coming with you guys, and none of my work is that important, this time of year. Things don't completely shut down during winter break, but very little that we do can't wait."

"You must do as you see best, of course, but reading the dean's email is likely to be quite boring," he said. That it was also likely to be even more disillusioning than what she heard already he didn't say.

"It's okay. I'm not trying to stick myself in. Do you have my cell number in case you want me for anything?"

"No."

"Here, just give me your phone and I'll put it in."

He complied, though with a little reluctance. She was very fast at it, despite also snapping a quick picture of herself for the address book entry, and returned the phone to him a few moments later.

She then gave them directions to the computer services building.

"See you later," she said.

"God be with you," Brother Thomas replied. Brother Francis let that suffice for him and gave a small wave.

Sonia smiled indulgently, then turned in the direction of

her office and walked briskly off.

"Protecting her?" Brother Francis asked when she was out of earshot.

"She doesn't need protection," Brother Thomas said.

"She seems surprisingly innocent," Francis said.

"She graduated recently, and hasn't been working in the administrative side for long," Brother Thomas said.

"What was her degree in?" Brother Francis asked.

"Math. Differential Analysis, specifically, if you know what that is," Brother Thomas said.

Brother Francis didn't bother answering the second part. Though he didn't know what Differential Analysis was, it wasn't very relevant to why he asked.

"She's still rather innocent for someone that intelligent," he said.

"One of the dangers of being pretty?" Brother Thomas suggested.

"It's certainly possible. People tend to be on their best behavior around good looking people. That could give someone a distorted view of how humanity actually behaves," Brother Francis replied.

"I take it the cynical explanation for that is obvious?" Brother Thomas asked.

Brother Francis smiled.

"At the same time, ugliness is a corruption of the human ideal and beauty reminds us of heaven. To sin you must forget goodness and beauty makes that forgetfulness harder. That's also why good looking liars are so dangerous. We know on an intuitive level that beauty should be united with truth," said Brother Francis.

"And so it should," Brother Thomas said.

"There's much that should be, but isn't, in this world,"

Bother Francis agreed.

"Since truth is beautiful, people assume that beauty is truthful; since beauty shines on the world, it is only natural that it sees a brighter world," Brother Thomas summarized.

Brother Francis smiled.

"I still haven't learned to get used to poetry from you," he said.

"Don't," Brother Thomas replied.

Francis chuckled.

"Getting back to your question," Brother Thomas continued, "She doesn't need protection—I suspect her innocence is doing her more harm than good, though not much of either—I was just telling the literal truth. We don't need her help, and I don't think that reading through the dean's email would be a good use of her time."

"Will it be a good use of our time?" Brother Francis asked.

Brother Thomas knew Brother Francis too well to take that as questioning his judgment.

"I'm not sure," Brother Thomas said. "On the one hand, one expects that to justify a murder there must be some profound motive. Something like sleeping with someone's wife, or like the provost's idea of a criminal who Floden sent to prison for twenty years. On the other hand, I think that there is something to Ian's warning that the narrowness of the academic world makes everything in it take on tremendous importance to the people trapped in that world."

"That's really true of all sin," Brother Francis said.

"True enough, but elaborate?" Brother Thomas said.

"Since sin is becoming less than yourself, as you become smaller, everything around you looks bigger. Sin and perspective are, necessarily, enemies."

Brother Thomas nodded in appreciation.

"I'm inclined to discount the fights that Dean Floden got into on the last day that he was seen alive, simply because they were academic, and thus not worth killing over. In that case, his email will probably be more illuminating, assuming that he used it as his private email like so many people do. On the other hand, since all murderers necessarily have perspective problems, his earlier meetings might well be more significant than his email."

"I suppose we can but see what we find," said Brother Francis.

"That's all anyone can do," Brother Thomas replied.

When they arrived at the computing services building, they had a little difficulty finding the man they were looking for. There were several people named Steven there and the person working the help desk did not have as strong an intuition of who the provost would have called as Brother Thomas had expected him to. After trying all three Stevens, the third turned out to be the one.

"Do you each want a computer to look at Floden's email, or are you going to read it together?" Steven asked, when they had come behind the reception desk and back into the main part of the building.

"If we could each have a computer, that would be more convenient. I expect that there will be a lot of email to sort through, so being able to divide the labor will be beneficial," Brother Thomas said.

"Sure, not a problem," Steven said.

He took them to a small office room which was divided into cubicles, most of which were unoccupied.

"You're not going to need to send email or edit files, right? Because setting up new accounts is a pain in the neck. You wouldn't believe how much paperwork we need to have filled out and approved to do it," Steven said.

"Read-only access to the network will be sufficient," Brother Thomas said.

"It's not that formal. We have a guest administrator account which we use for consultants. I'm just going to trust you guys that you're not going to do anything with it but read Floden's email."

"We won't do anything besides that," Brother Thomas promised.

Steven booted up the computers, logged them in, and opened Dean Floden's email account. It turned out that he was one of those people who never file or delete anything. His inbox had twenty-three thousand emails in it dating back over fifteen years.

"I'll take the last week and you take the week before?" Brother Thomas said.

"Okay," said Brother Francis.

It was immediately evident that Jack Floden was not too cautious to use his work email for private conversations. Both brothers discovered that Tiffany Clinton was correct about the nature of the relationship between Dean Floden and Audrey, whose last name turned out to be Flanagan. Tiffany's characterization of his manner with faculty turned out also to be correct, at least over email. His tone might be described as stern, but if he wasn't nice, equally he was not antagonistic.

It took about an hour to go through the first two weeks of his email, and when they finished, the brothers took a break and found a private place to discuss their results.

"I found a few things that might be worth looking into further, but I'm very curious as to your impression of Floden based on his emails," Brother Thomas said.

"Contradictory," Brother Francis said. "On the one hand, there is a man who is reasonably circumspect with his colleagues. On the other hand, he is most indiscreet with his private life. To be practical in defiance of morality is common enough. What's odd is that he doesn't seem to be moral in the ways that practicality encourages. Sexual scandals in general won't ruin careers the way they used to, say, fifty years ago, but sexual relationships with subordinates and students will. And he makes reference to both in his emails."

"Do you think he was one of those people who are just convinced of their own invulnerability?" Brother Thomas asked.

"No doubt he at least strongly suspected it, but I think he probably courted danger to make himself feel alive. The thrill of sending off an email you know you shouldn't proves that you're not dead yet. The modern world has revised Descartes: I feel, therefore I am."

"In fairness to the modern world, that's not very different from Martin Luther's 'I feel saved, therefore I am saved,'" Brother Thomas said.

"I suppose, though only if you don't side with Chesterton in saying that Martin Luther began the modern world," Brother Francis said.

"Even if you do, Luther died before Descartes was born. The modern world could hardly revise what came after it," Brother Thomas said.

"If the whole world were a single thing, that would be true. But the world is made up of many people, and there's nothing to prevent Descartes from being a throwback to an earlier age. Given that he was trying to establish the validity of sense data, and consequently the usefulness of reason, that's actually a pretty safe assumption," Brother Francis said.

"Fair enough," Thomas said.

"Getting back to your question, the other thing about Floden is that he seemed lonely. I know that must come as a shock—what with the popularity that unpleasant people usually enjoy—but even so, he seemed to be often reaching out in small ways, indirectly asking people if they liked him. I don't know how that would play out in person."

"Let's read further back, and see whether it's consistent, and of course whether any events stand out as significant," Brother Thomas said.

Brother Francis nodded.

They spent several more hours reading the Dean's email, increasingly skipping around. They covered most of the previous year by the time the building closed for the day.

President Blendermore had invited them to dinner at his house, and they decided to accept. They walked there, taking a short a detour to look at Marduk Hall at night. It was a good looking building, though not imposing, and at night the ivy which covered most of the front took on a slightly ominous look. The street lights were on the other side, which illuminated the sidewalk well enough but left the building largely in shadow.

A thought occurred to Brother Francis.

"Do you think that someone might be able to climb down from the Dean's Office? It would explain the open windows," he said.

"I don't know, which is why I texted Michael a picture this morning to see what he thought," Brother Thomas said.

"And?" Brother Francis asked.

"He said he couldn't tell from a picture."

Brother Francis rolled his eyes, but discreetly.

"If you're waiting for me to laugh, please proceed as if I

have," he said.

"Fortunately, he was able to have one of his black sashes cover for him, and will join us tomorrow morning to look for himself."

"That's very generous," Brother Francis said.

"It is," Brother Thomas concurred.

At dinner, the brothers discovered that between Ian and Staci, it was Ian who did all of the cooking. Owing to his time constraints, he was a big fan of their slow cooker. On this night, he had made osso bucco in red wine, with lightly steamed green beans in butter on the side.

"How have the investigations been going?" Ian asked.

"Well, so far," Brother Thomas said.

"Is it possible to tell whether you've made any progress?" Ian asked.

"Not really. There's much we've found out, but whether it will lead to the truth is not possible to know before it leads us there," Brother Thomas said.

"Has Sonia been helpful?" Staci asked.

"Very," Brother Thomas said.

"She's a good girl," Staci said.

"She's not that young, you know. She has a PhD," Ian said.

Staci smiled.

"Age is just a number, my dear. She may have celebrated twenty-six or twenty-seven birthdays, but she's more innocent and trusting than most eighteen-year-old's I've known. I really want to know how she's managed that being as pretty as she is."

None of the men in the room were willing to touch that

comment with a ten foot pole, so she answered it herself.

"Of course, she studied math. I don't mean that ridiculous idea about intelligence in a woman being a turn-off. Plenty of men are attracted to intelligent women. I mean that it seems like all math people are introverts. It's amazing how much attention a woman can avoid without realizing it by looking uninviting."

No one was willing to touch that with a ten foot pole either.

"So how did you find Tiffany?" she asked.

Brother Thomas and Brother Francis exchanged glances. Staci was apparently feeling mischievous.

"Sonia led us to her," Brother Thomas said with intentional literalism.

Staci laughed.

Brother Thomas smiled slightly, then answered the real question.

"She helped us."

"Willingly?" Staci asked.

Brother Thomas hesitated.

"Yes."

"You'll have to share your technique. That's more than most of us can get out of her," Staci said.

"It did take a little persuasion," Brother Thomas admitted.

"Brother Thomas pointed out that we were preferable to the police, and with help might cut the police investigation short," Brother Francis said.

Staci smiled.

"Will you be having Sonia show you around more tomorrow? I think she was disappointed when you sent her back to the office," Ian said.

"Reading through somebody's email isn't nearly as interesting as it sounds," Brother Thomas said.

"The interesting emails never have descriptive subjects, so you have to read through everything. Deans send and receive a great deal of mundane email!" Brother Francis explained.

Ian laughed.

"If you think deans receive a lot of mundane email, you should see *my* inbox!" he said.

"To answer your question, yes, I think we'll be interviewing a number of people tomorrow, for which Sonia's help will be invaluable," Brother Thomas said.

"By the way, did you talk with Martha—the provost?" Ian asked.

"We did," Thomas said.

"How did she take your presence here?" Ian asked.

"She was very practical about it. I think she views us as possibly useful and more cooperative at least than the police—where the best interests of the university are concerned. She was the one who gave us permission to read Dean Floden's email," Brother Thomas said.

"That's good. I don't need her approval, but it's convenient to have it," Ian said.

"Why didn't you tell her about us?" Brother Francis asked.

"It's easier to ask for forgiveness than permission. It's also easier to give forgiveness than permission," he said.

"Those might be related," Staci said.

"No doubt they are," Ian said.

Chapter 6

In the morning, after a quick breakfast, Brother Thomas and Brother Francis arrived at the president's office promptly at nine o'clock, but Sonia was there before them.

"Hi!" she said when they entered.

They both returned her greeting.

"I figured that there were a lot of people you would want to talk to today, so I came in a little early to clear out the work I had to do. I should be fine even if you need me all day."

Brother Francis smiled.

"Thank you," Brother Thomas said.

"So who are we going to go see first?" Sonia asked.

"I would like to see if we can talk with Audrey," Brother Thomas said.

"That might be a bit delicate," Sonia said.

"It would be awkward for her if we were to visit her at her lab, seeing as how she shouldn't have any connection to Dean Floden. If young people today actually checked their email I would suggest emailing her. In default of that, is there any chance you could make up some plausible official reason for calling her, and arrange a meeting?"

Sonia smiled.

"I can think of something. Perhaps I'll ask her to come here because Ian wants some potential donors to meet some students, who we've picked at random. That has actually happened before, though we haven't told anyone about it so it's not like its plausibility would be widely known. On the other hand, it is the sort of thing that presidents' offices do. If she goes with it, no one would have any reason to doubt it."

The brothers made no objection, and Sonia picked up the phone. She had been looking up Audrey's office number while she was talking.

"Ian won't mind us using him for cover like this," she said as she dialed the numbers.

She waited until someone picked up.

"Hi, this is Sonia Olivera calling for President Blendermore. Is Audrey Flanagan there? I'd like to speak to her related to an alumni outreach program. Thanks."

Brother Thomas appreciated the way that Sonia carefully pronounced Audrey's last name, as if it were the first time she was reading it off of a list.

"Hello, Audrey? Hi, this is Sonia Olivera from the president's office. Are you reasonably alone? Okay, we'll keep this to yes or no questions. This is going to be awkward, so I'm just going to come out and say it. I'm calling with some detectives who are working for the president investigating Dean Floden's death, and we know that you and he... spent time together. Can you come to the president's office to talk to them? You can use the cover story of meeting an alumni donor as part of fundraising efforts, if you like. Thank you."

She hung up the phone.

"She'll be here in about ten minutes."

"How did she take the request?" Brother Francis asked.

"She was surprised, of course," Sonia said.

"Was she scared?" he asked.

"I don't think so. She was a little hesitant, but I think only because the phone call was a little out of left field," she said.

Audrey arrived in about fifteen minutes. She was a tall, skinny blonde, who was twenty-two and looked it. Her hair was slightly below shoulder length, straight, and cut with a few layers with side-swept bangs. Her clothes were a compromise between practicality and style. They leaned a little more towards the stylish side, and certainly wouldn't leave the impression that her figure wasn't worth showing off.

Ian was out, so they used his office and closed the door.

"Please, sit down," Sonia said. Since they were using her boss's office, she felt like she should be hospitable.

Audrey sat down, and looked from person to person.

"This is Brother Thomas, and Brother Francis," Sonia said.

They shook hands.

Brother Thomas waited a moment, then began.

"As Dr. Olivera said on the phone, we're aware of the nature of your relationship with Dean Floden. Given the mysterious nature of what happened to him, we're reaching out to everyone who knew him to see if they can tell us anything about him that might help us figure out what happened," he said.

"I see," Audrey said.

"I'd offer my condolences, but I don't want to insult you," he added.

"I see you know the nature of our 'relationship'," Audrey said. She moved her head in a manner that was expressive, perhaps of defiance, though it was unclear since it was almost certainly cribbed from television.

Brother Thomas nodded.

"Were you exclusive?" Brother Francis asked.

"No. Though I don't have anyone else right now. I broke up with my last boyfriend about six months ago, and have been taking it easy since school is a lot of work right now—I've got qualifying exams coming up," she said.

"How did your relationship start?" Brother Thomas asked.

"If you can even call it a relationship. I'd say that we were friends with benefits, except that we weren't friends. I'm not sure what you'd call it, exactly," she said.

"Most of the terms are colorful, and we don't need a label," Brother Thomas said.

Audrey laughed.

"You're really not like what I thought monks would be like."

"We're not monks," Brother Thomas said.

"Then why the get-up?" she asked.

"We're friars."

"What's the difference?"

"I don't think you'd care about the technical details, but suffice it to say calling us monks would be like calling you a physicist because you're in grad school."

"No offense," she said, defensively.

"None taken."

"What did you want to know?" she said with a hint of impatience in her voice.

"How did you and the dean come to the arrangement you had?" Brother Thomas asked.

"He was a biology professor," she said.

She paused, considering what level of detail to go into.

"I took a class he taught my first semester of grad school.

He flirted with me and I liked it. He was a decent looking guy, and I enjoyed how much he was into me. I mean, he could have lost his job if people found out about us. It was flattering that I had that power over him, you know? I liked it. It made me feel sexy. And he was very attentive. And, you know, it was kind of nice that I didn't have to worry about grades and stuff because I knew he'd help me out if I needed it."

Sonia shuddered, though only Brother Thomas saw it.

"When did you last see Dean Floden?" Brother Thomas asked.

"The Friday before he was found," Audrey said.

"Which part of the day?"

"That evening. I came over to his place. Do you want all the details?" she asked.

"Are any of the details pertinent to how Dean Floden died?" Brother Thomas asked.

"I don't think so," she said.

"Then no, we don't want all the details. Did you spend the night there?"

"No. I never do. We have our fun, then I get on with my life. It's not like we would cuddle afterwards," she said.

"Did Dean Floden ever want you to stay?" Brother Francis asked.

"He never asked me to. At first he was embarrassed about it. I think he thought I expected it, or something. I took a shower and left, and he was relieved. That's pretty much how it always went."

"Is that how it went on Friday?" Brother Thomas asked.

"Yeah," she said.

"Do you have any idea what time it was when you left? And, for that matter, when you got there?"

"I was supposed to meet him at six, and I don't think that I was late. Let me check my phone and I can tell you when I left, because I got a call while I was in the bathroom, as I was—

"Right before I left," she rephrased.

She pulled out her phone and started looking through it. After about forty-five seconds, she started to type and it became apparent that she had gotten distracted by someone texting her. Brother Thomas wasn't overly concerned; he had already gotten most of what he expected out of the witness.

"It's only by a few hours, but this does extend the last time he was seen alive," Brother Thomas said to Brother Francis.

"It also places him at home, after work was finished—especially considering the early closing—before he ended up in his office, dead. I really wonder what might have made him go back, if in fact he was killed there," Brother Francis said.

"I think he was killed there. For one thing, dragging a corpse around would be more than a little conspicuous. You could try to pass it off as helping a drunk friend, as long as no one came close, but that's awfully risky, and for no obvious benefit. Granted, less risky at night during a snowstorm, assuming of course that he was killed on Friday. Even so, I'm inclined to side with Raymond Chandler. Dead men are heavier than broken hearts."

"What does that mean?" Sonia asked.

"Not much," Brother Thomas admitted. "In The Big Sleep, it meant that someone had to have had a significant reason for moving a corpse, since it's not easy work. Of course, you also have to have a significant reason for moving a corpse since it's illegal, immoral, and involves you touching a corpse. Frankly, the weight of the corpse is probably one of the lesser reasons for not moving it."

"What does that have to do with Dean Floden?" Sonia asked.

"Very little. Philip Marlowe knew that the corpse was moved, and deduced from it that the person who moved him thought it important, since a corpse is heavy. Of course, it later turned out that the corpse was moved less than thirty feet, which rendered unsound his carefully reasoned deduction of the obvious. We're working in the other direction: if the corpse was moved, it would have been moved quite far, and there's no obvious reason to do it. Therefore, I suspect that the corpse wasn't moved."

This conversation had the effect of recalling Audrey to why she had pulled her phone out in the first place, and she looked up the time of that call.

"I got the call at seven fifteen, so I left at like seven twenty or maybe seven twenty-five," she said.

"Where did you go?" Brother Thomas asked.

"I went back to my apartment, then I went out with some friends for dinner," she said.

"Did Dean Floden seem to be in good spirits when you left?" Brother Thomas asked.

Audrey looked at him like she couldn't believe what she heard.

"If you're asking if I'm good in bed, yes, very," she said in a tone which was equal parts patronizing and offended.

"I wasn't asking that at all," Brother Thomas said.

"Then what?" she said.

"Did he seem at all preoccupied, worried, like there was something on his mind?" Brother Thomas asked.

"Oh. No. I don't think so," she said.

"Did you hear from him after that?" Brother Thomas asked.

"No," she said.

"Was that unusual?"

"It would depend on his mood. Usually we would get together more on weekends, but not always."

"You said that you and he were not exclusive. Did you know of any other sexual partners he had?" Brother Thomas asked.

"We didn't talk about his personal life. He tried a few times, but I shut that down. I didn't care, and I didn't want to hear about his problems," she said.

"Do you know what drugs he was fond of?" Brother Thomas said.

"How would I know?" she asked.

"You never did them together?"

"Sometimes he would get some weed for me, but I never did anything heavier than that with him."

"You spent time in his house and in his bathroom. Did you ever see anything besides marijuana?" he asked.

"No," she said.

"Did the dean ever help you out?"

"How do you mean? With money?" she asked, surprised.

"No. You mentioned before that part of the allure of the relationship for you was that he was in a position to help you out academically if you ever needed it. Did you?" Brother Thomas asked.

"Actually, no," she said, and chuckled as she thought about it from that perspective. "Grad school wasn't as hard as I expected it to be."

Brother Thomas noticed Sonia struggling, successfully, to keep from rolling her eyes. A shadow of a smile crossed his lips for a moment. He drew out a business card and handed it to Audrey.

"Thank you for your help. If you come across anything that might help us in clearing up this matter, please get in touch," Brother Thomas said.

"I will," Audrey said in a manner which suggested that she probably wouldn't.

"One other question, if I may," Brother Francis said.

"Yes?"

"If the dean hadn't died, how long do you think your relationship with him, such as it was, would have lasted?"

Audrey shrugged her shoulders.

"I don't know. I'd have ended it for a serious boyfriend. Otherwise... I guess it would have kept on going until I graduated," she said.

"Thank you," he said.

Sonia opened the door for Audrey without saying anything. Audrey looked at Sonia, who was an inch shorter, then changed her expression. Catty was probably the most accurate description.

"Do you enjoy being better than everyone else?" she asked in a tone which admitted no doubt of the answer.

Sonia, who had significantly overestimated how subtle her reactions during the interview were, was caught by surprise and didn't know what to say.

Audrey turned to Brother Thomas and said, "It was nice meeting you."

She then blew him a kiss and walked out. Sonia stared openly at her, though Audrey didn't notice since she didn't look back. Brother Thomas laughed softly.

Sonia closed the door.

"What a whore!"

"I doubt very much that she trades sex for money," Brother Thomas said.

"I didn't mean it literally," Sonia said.

"I know. I was trying to suggest that it is a term best left to its literal meaning."

"Why? Because that would be judging her?"

"I wouldn't put it that way, but yes."

"What's wrong with judging her? The facts are pretty clear. We heard them from her."

"I'm not saying that you should suspend judgment on what she did. Her actions, in themselves, were clearly bad. But you'll be happier if you hold off on judging *her*. Neither you nor I nor even she knows enough to do that accurately."

"What, is there supposed to be some way she could not know what she was doing? I mean, look at how she walked out. She was flirting with you. And even if she doesn't know the difference between a monk and a friar, she's got to know enough to know that was completely inappropriate."

"Of course she knew. But that wasn't directed at me."

"There was no one behind you," Sonia said.

"Obviously she blew a kiss at me. I mean I wasn't the audience for it. That is, it wasn't for my sake that she did that," he said.

"Then why did she do it?" she asked.

"To antagonize you," he said.

Sonia blushed, though it was subtle underneath her olive skin.

"Are you saying that she was trying to make me jealous?" she said incredulously.

"No. Not at all. It was not a specific gesture. I mean, it was directed at me, but I wasn't personally relevant to it. A great deal of what women do with men doesn't have to do with the men, *specifically*. It could have been anyone—as long as it was a male—as far as she was concerned."

"How could it not matter who you were?"

"She noticed you disapproving of her, and wanted to unsettle you. One of the great truths of life is that it doesn't matter nearly as much what you have as how you use it. Weaker but more aggressive people routinely win in fights. Less attractive but more determined women often succeed in attracting men. If you'll permit me to avoid discussing your relative beauty as not well suited to propriety—and in any event you've seen her and can easily enough find a mirror if you've never looked in one before—you clearly are more morally pure. If you'll pardon my using the term, and only for the sake of brevity, she's a slut and you're not, which would rank her below you if all other things were equal. She wanted to prove they're not. The fact that you two are not in competition over me is irrelevant. All she wanted to demonstrate was that if you were, she would win."

Sonia furrowed her brows as she considered that.

"How does that make what she did okay?" she asked at last.

"I'm not saying that it was okay, I'm saying that she was defending herself, rather than being aggressive without provocation. In some ways, she was telling you to back off because she already knew what you were telling her."

"I didn't say anything!" Sonia said.

"The way you opened the door without saying anything, and how you looked at her were eloquent enough," he said.

Sonia sighed.

"She's still a slut."

"I dislike the term, but I don't think that even Audrey would disagree with you. At least if she didn't think you were attacking her by saying it," he said.

"Perhaps. But I am attacking her by saying it. She shouldn't sleep around to feel powerful and keep blackmail in her back pocket," Sonia said.

"You're right, she shouldn't," he said.

"Then what's the problem?"

"She is not her actions. By all means condemn the actions, but don't condemn her along with them."

"But she did them," Sonia said.

"Yes, but that's not all she did. She's done many things, plenty of them good. It is a great mistake to blaspheme something good because of something else good. In this case, it would be a terrible mistake to blaspheme the good things that Audrey has done because of the good things she hasn't done. Even though the good things she hasn't done are extremely good things like chastity, honesty, and charity."

"What good things has she done?" Sonia said.

"For the most part, neither you nor I know. But it is inexcusable to confuse ignorance with knowledge of nonexistence. And trivially, she's kept herself alive instead of killing herself."

"Most people don't kill themselves. Why should she get a medal for it?" she asked.

"Have you considered that perhaps most people *should* get a medal for not killing themselves? That a virtue is common does not make it a vice. A person doesn't have to be in the top ten percent of human beings for their life to have worth."

"I didn't say that her life was worthless," Sonia said.

"Then I suppose we agree," Brother Thomas said.

"I don't think so, but I'm not sure why not," Sonia said.

"The main difference is in the question of how you would treat repentance, I think," said Brother Francis.

Sonia looked at him, waiting for him to explain.

74

"When you identify the sinner with the sin, as in calling Audrey a slut, you tend to be very resistant to accepting it if she repents. Whatever she does, she's has been a slut, and should be treated as a slut. Of course, you can always say that she can change. In that case saying that she is a slut is nothing more than saying she has, in the past, done slutty things. But that's not how the verb 'to be' works in the English language. Whatever you might mean, your meaning will become colored by the words you used to say it. Say that a woman has done bad things, and you will much more readily accept her changing her ways than if you say that she is a woman who does bad things."

Sonia mulled this over. As she did so, Brother Thomas's phone beeped, indicating that he received a text. He pulled his phone out and read the message.

"Saved by the bell," he said. He turned to Brother Francis, "It's Michael—he's here."

Chapter 7

Sonia gave Brother Thomas a quizzical look.

"Is this bad?" she asked.

"No, it's good," Brother Thomas answered. "Michael Chesterton is a friend of ours.

He's come, at my request, to consult about the possibility of climbing up to or down

from the dean's window. He's a most interesting man. I think that you'll like him."

"Is he a friar like you?" Sonia asked.

"No, he's not a friar of any kind. He is living the committed single life, but he's

made no vows to any religious order," Brother Thomas said.

"How did he get here so early in the morning?" Brother Francis asked.

"He said that he made part of the trip last night and stayed with a friend, so he only

had about half the trip to make this morning," Brother Thomas answered.

"Where is he now?" Sonia asked.

"In Parking Lot C," Brother Thomas said. "Let's go pick him up then take him to Marduk Hall."

Parking Lot C was not the closest parking lot, but it did have the virtue of not requiring a permit. They found Michael easily since his was very nearly the only car in the lot.

At six-foot-four, Michael Chesterton was a tall man. Winter coats reveal little about a person, but he looked to have an athletic build. He moved with the assured grace of someone used to using his body with precision in all circumstances. He was a similar age to Brother Thomas, but his eyes, while also brown, if perhaps a shade darker brown, were a marked contrast to those of Brother Thomas. Whereas Brother Thomas's eyes were alert and piercing, almost hungry, Michael's were calm and almost serene. The rest of his face was handsome, though not beautiful. While Taylor Swift would never write a song about it, when not otherwise engaged, it wore a mixture of confidence and kindness which was pleasant to look at.

"Hello, Thomas!" he said cheerfully, while they were still some ways off, and waved. His voice fit his large body. It was deep and full, though not so much that you would expect it to say "In a world..." at the beginning of a movie trailer.

When they got closer, he greeted Francis too, and Brother Thomas introduced Sonia. They shook hands, and it felt to Sonia like shaking granite. Having done rock climbing for a few years herself, she recognized it as the grip of a life-long climber. Presumably sailors in the 1800s would have had hands like that too but in the modern world it was a mostly unique phenomenon.

"Thank you for getting here so quickly," Brother Thomas said.

"It was no great effort, and it was pleasant to spend an

evening with Rob and his family outside of hunting season," Michael said.

"Does he have children?" Brother Francis asked.

"Yes, two girls: six and two. The elder just started learning to shoot a bow like her father. The younger has recently figured out how to play games on the iPad, and heaven help the person whose job it is to persuade her to put it down," he said.

Brother Thomas nodded and turned to Sonia.

"Would you lead the way to Marduk Hall? We might as well go to it directly."

"Sure," she said, and began walking.

They walked in a loose formation, more or less side by side, and didn't talk much. Brother Thomas was thinking about the case, Sonia was feeling a little shy, Brother Francis was speculating about human nature, and Michael was content with silence and looking at a new place. They walked briskly, and came to Marduk Hall in ten minutes.

"Here it is," Sonia said, when they had come in front of it.

"To a window, or to the top?" Michael asked.

"To that window," Thomas said, pointing at the dean's office.

Michael walked up and looked at the brickwork, then at the ivy covering the front of the building. He backed up a little, examining the brickwork progressively further up. He walked closer again and tested some of the ivy.

He then began climbing the brickwork, near a lower window, taking advantage of some of the protrusions around it. He was up to the dean's window in about twenty seconds. He paused, considered, then down-climbed it in less than a minute.

"The bricks are set fairly evenly, but there are a lot of places where the mortar has decayed, giving decent finger and toe holds. V1 to V2, depending on the height, arm span, hand size, and shoes of the climber. It would take someone who has climbed, but not necessarily very much, depending on their natural strength-to-weight ratio. I haven't tried the ivy, but I wouldn't want to rely on it, myself. Someone under one hundred twenty pounds would probably be willing to try it," he said.

"Would you have seen any evidence that someone had climbed it recently?" Brother Thomas asked.

"No. Not unless they chalked up for it, which would be unlikely in cold weather," Michael said.

Brother Thomas considered.

"I presume that you're thinking that a strange person might have come into the building, making the murderer panic and go out the window?" Michael asked.

Brother Thomas nodded.

"That would be more difficult, since they wouldn't have checked out the holds beforehand. It would also argue for shoes unsuited for climbing. Most winter boots would be awful for climbing in. Both would mean a more experienced climber," Michael said.

Brother Thomas considered this.

"Of course, a person might have opened the windows just to see whether they could get out that way, then decided not to and left the windows open because they didn't care," Michael observed.

They contemplated the building silently for a few moments.

"Is your preferred theory that the windows were left open to hide the time of death? No one can have an alibi for every moment of several days?" Michael asked.

"It seems the most likely explanation," Brother Thomas said, without conviction.

Michael nodded.

"Do you mind if I stick around with you for a while? There's nowhere I have to be, and it's been some time since I've had the pleasure of your company."

"You would be exceedingly welcome," said Brother Thomas.

"Who should we talk to next?" Brother Francis asked.

"Actually, I think we're better off heading for mass. It's a little early, but if we went to interview someone, we would probably have to cut it short, which I would rather not do," Brother Thomas said.

He turned to Sonia.

"You're welcome to come with us, of course," he said.

"Thank you. I think I will," she said.

Brother Thomas started walking in the direction of the church, then paused.

"We have a few minutes, and it just occurred to me that if the police didn't search the office very thoroughly, the same might apply to the grounds," he said.

"The ground underneath the window showed no footprints," Michael said.

"We might as well search carefully as walk to church slowly," Brother Thomas said.

In front of the building there were several large rhododendrons, their leaves rolled to resist the cold weather. There was one directly below the dean's window. Brother Thomas looked at it, starting from the top, which was about five feet high, and worked his way down. When he was still three feet off the ground, he paused, then stood up and gestured for the others to come. He pushed a branch aside and pointed.

There, stuck in one of the branches, was a hypodermic needle. When everyone had taken a look, Brother Thomas took several pictures of the needle using his phone and continued the search.

He found a second needle lying on the ground. He gave the others the opportunity to look, then photographed it too.

"I would say that was time well spent," he said.

"The police don't seem to have been very thorough," Brother Francis said.

"Possibly just not very imaginative, but those are not exclusive. I doubt that they've had any murders in recent memory, and this isn't the time of year when one naturally wants to exert oneself. I don't mean that they haven't been diligent, but Christmastime does not lend itself to examining the shrubbery," Brother Thomas said.

"I know *I'm* getting cold," Sonia said.

"Exactly," Brother Thomas said.

"It will be interesting to meet the sheriff," Brother Francis said.

"Indeed. Well, shall we go to the church now? We'll still be early, but the extra time might be well spent giving thanks," Brother Thomas said.

"That's always a good use of time," Michael said.

They walked to the church, without haste, but were still about fifteen minutes early. Brother Thomas, Brother Francis, and Michael kneeled in prayer. After about a minute Michael sat down, though he seemed to continue praying. Sonia found it a little awkward, though less than she thought she should, and passed the time looking at the stained glass windows. The church was almost one hundred years old and built in a style that aped a cathedral. Perhaps it would be better to say paid tribute to a cathedral. Either way that meant that there was a lot of beauty crammed into a relatively small space. It was enough to keep one's attention for a quarter of an hour.

Sonia found the mass very curious, in no small part because Michael seemed to be at least as devout as the brothers. If intelligent people taking something seriously that common people also took seriously was a novelty to her the day before, someone (comparatively) young and good looking, in good health, and with well developed social skills taking it seriously was perhaps a bigger shock. Not that there was anything wrong with Brother Thomas or Brother Francis, but after all they were brothers and in a sense being religious was their job. In many ways, the thing that makes religious expression by those in religious life acceptable to secular people is thinking of their beliefs as part of their job rather than part of them. If she had thought about it, she would have realized that didn't mean anything because they chose that life with their eyes open, when it was not their job. But she didn't think about it, and the human tendency to pigeonhole people had won out. But none of this applied to Michael. He was someone who, in an earthly sense, had no need of the church. And yet he was there anyway. This didn't lead anywhere in Sonia's thoughts, it just popped up more than a few times during mass.

* * *

When mass was over, Brother Thomas said that he wanted to talk to the other people who saw Dean Floden on Friday. Interviewing them in chronological order was as good as any other way to do it, so he picked that. The first on the list was Dr. Frank Buskirk, a professor in the psychology department.

He wasn't at his office, so they looked up his home address. It was only a twenty minute walk from the psychology building so they went there in search of him. They had to knock a few times, but eventually he answered the door. He was on the shorter side of average, with medium-length hair and a short, pointy beard which looked like it might be compensating for a lack of muscle mass.

"Hello?" he said. His tone was hesitant, though polite. Possibly he saw the brothers' habits and assumed they were some sort of cult trying to proselytize him.

"Hello, Dr. Buskirk?" Sonia said. Since she was the only one present who was actually connected to the university, introductions were her job, even off of school property.

"Yes?" he said.

"My name is Sonia Olivera. I work for President Blendermore. These are Brother Thomas and Brother Francis, and their associate Michael Chesterton. The brothers are looking into the death of Dean Floden, on behalf of the university."

"Oh!" he said.

Something more would have been appropriate, but he didn't add anything.

"We've come to see you because you spoke with Dean Floden on the last day he was seen alive," said Brother Thomas. "We're trying to piece together what happened on that day, and were hoping that you could tell us about your meeting with the dean."

"I see," Dr. Buskirk said.

He looked like he was still fearful that at any moment they might ask him if he had accepted Jesus as his personal Lord and Savior.

"Do you remember when you met with Dean Floden on Friday?" Brother Thomas asked.

"Was it Friday? I thought maybe it was Thursday," Dr. Buskirk said.

"Dean Floden's secretary remembers it as being Friday, sir," Brother Thomas said.

"If you say so. I don't remember it well—I wasn't there long," Dr. Buskirk said.

"What did you talk about?" Brother Thomas asked.

Dr. Buskirk paused, and looked thoughtful. Then his face cleared up.

"Oh, right. He asked me to step in for a minute because one of my grad students thought he caught a student cheating. Jack wanted my opinion because grad students—especially new grad students—can leap to conclusions. Which is what happened here. I looked into it, and the students were just study partners. So I told him I didn't think it warranted his involvement after all, and that was it."

"And how did he seem to you that day?" Brother Thomas asked.

"What do you mean?" Dr. Buskirk replied.

"Did he seem worried? Nervous? Preoccupied? Happy?"

"Oh. I see. Maybe a little worried or preoccupied. He seemed relieved at not having to deal with the plagiarism issue. Though to tell you the truth, I don't think it would have mattered very much to him either way," Dr. Buskirk said.

"Oh?" Brother Thomas asked.

Dr. Buskirk seemed a little taken aback.

"I just mean that he had been a dean a long time, and was used to its duties," he said.

"Oh, of course," Brother Thomas said.

"Is there anything else I can help you with?" Dr. Buskirk

asked.

"I don't think so," Brother Thomas said.

"I have one question, if you don't mind," Brother Francis said.

Dr. Buskirk turned, annoyance covered by a careful exertion of politeness on his face.

"Yes?" he said.

"I was just wondering if you could hazard any guess as to why someone might want to kill the dean," Brother Francis said.

"I'm sorry, I can't," he said.

He thought about it for a moment, then seemed to think he should add something.

"I didn't really know Dean Floden well. He was a good dean and in my experience was generally nice to everyone who knew him professionally. What he did in his personal life, though, I couldn't say, since we were only professional acquaintances," he explained.

"Thank you," Brother Francis said.

"If that's all you need?" Dr. Buskirk said.

"Actually, I have a question," Michael said.

Dr. Buskirk sighed, slightly.

"Yes?" he said.

"What's your favorite color?" Michael said.

Dr. Buskirk blinked.

"I don't see how that's relevant."

"It's not," Michael said.

"Orange," Dr. Buskirk said.

"That explains the color of your mailbox," Michael said.

"Indeed. Good day, gentlemen. Miss," Dr. Buskirk said, waved farewell in a friendly way, and closed the door.

Dr. Buskirk's mailbox was blue.

As they were walking back to the road, Brother Thomas said, "Next, I believe, is Dr. Marten."

"Okay, if you're not going to ask about it, I will," Sonia said. "What was that about his favorite color, and how does it explain his mailbox being blue?"

"It doesn't," Michael said.

"Then why did you say it?" Sonia asked.

"I was curious whether Dr. Buskirk would make the same objection which you just did," he said.

"Why?" Sonia asked.

"Because he knew what was relevant to the investigation," Brother Thomas said.

"I'm curious why Dr. Buskirk is the only person on this campus who thinks that Dean Floden was kind and inoffensive," Brother Francis said.

"I'm more curious why he lied about what he went to see Dean Floden about," Brother Thomas said.

"How do you know he lied?" Sonia asked.

"I thoroughly read Dean Floden's email for the last month. There were three plagiarism complaints, but none from the psychology department. Dean Floden and Dr. Buskirk did exchange a few emails, though not about plagiarism. Dr. Buskirk was eligible for a grant if the university would reduce its overhead fee. Dean Floden wasn't exactly encouraging, though it seemed he was trying to help. The matter had not been completely resolved by last weekend and I doubt very much that Buskirk would show up in Dean Floden's office and not talk about it," Brother Thomas said.

They walked in silence to Dr. Marten's office in the English building. She turned out to be in, though she was meeting with a grad student when they got there. Sonia knocked on her door and let her know that they were waiting, then they settled down on some benches in the hallway.

Either the matter Dr. Marten was talking about was quite important, or she wasn't very concerned with her next visitors, because it took twenty minutes before the grad student—a twenty-five-year-old male of northern Indian descent, by the look of him—came out of her office. Sonia said hello as she passed him in the hallway, but he hurried past without looking at them.

"Good afternoon, Dr. Marten," Sonia said as she entered.

"Hello," Dr. Marten said.

She had straight brown hair cut in a somewhat severe bob and was wearing a very businesslike jacket which looked professional to the untrained eye. In an academic setting looked like nothing so much as overcompensation. Ordinarily she was a tolerably attractive woman, but she was plainly annoyed at her visitors and her face didn't wear annoyance well.

"This is Brother Thomas and Brother Francis. They're investigating Dean Floden's death on behalf of the university. And this is their associate, Michael," Sonia said.

"I don't approve of private detectives," Dr. Marten said.

"I don't approve of bad philosophy masquerading as literary criticism," Brother Thomas said.

Dr. Marten looked at him aghast.

"Is that an aspersion on my scholarship?" she demanded.

"Let us say, rather, that it refers to the papers you've published that I've read at least the first few pages of," Brother Thomas said.

Dr. Marten sat at her desk angrily trying to think of something to say.

"Doctor, I don't care whether or not I have your approval. It probably matters even less to me than whether *you* having *my* approval matters to you. What I do care about, and what you should care about, is the fact that we have a dead man, and don't know who killed him, and you were seen to have had a very heated argument with him the last day he was seen alive. You had a motive, and everyone on this campus had the opportunity. As the song goes, two out of three ain't bad."

"Are you saying that because I'm a woman and didn't just bow down and agree with a man, I must have killed him?" Dr. Marten asked.

Brother Thomas paused.

"Yes," he said, with as much sincerity as he could fake.

Dr. Marten was caught by surprise, and didn't say anything before Brother Thomas continued.

"All women who disagree with men murder them. You're a woman who disagreed with a man, therefore you murdered him. It's simple logic," he said, with conviction.

"That is so completely invalid!" Dr. Marten said.

"Actually, it's completely valid. What it is not, is sound. Validity refers only to the quality of the logic; soundness, to that together with the truth of the premises," he said.

"You know what I meant," Dr. Marten said.

"I don't, but I don't care. Here's the thing: I suspect you because nobody is as dumb as you're currently pretending to be. I know you're not a genius, but you're not this dumb. You're not drunk, and you're not high on anything. The only reason that sober people seem this much stupider than they actually are is because they're hiding something-"

Dr. Marten started to interrupt, but Brother Thomas interrupted her back.

"Hold on. I'm almost done and you'll be a lot better off if you let me finish. I don't know what you're hiding, and if you did kill Dean Floden, your best bet would seem to be to tell me nothing. But that raises a problem: if you tell me nothing, it tells me that you did kill him. And unless you managed to pull off the perfect crime, which would be odd for your first time, with the police and us doing our best to prove that you did it, you don't stand much of a chance. The more you try to get rid of me, the more I'm going to dedicate my life to making yours miserable. So your best course of action, in reality, is to cut out the bluffing and tell me what I want to know."

"How dare you talk to me like that?" Dr. Marten said, only half choking back rage.

"Because you have no power over me, and I don't care what you think of me," Brother Thomas said.

"This is completely intolerable," she spat.

"I know. And yet I didn't punch you in the face. Sometimes we must tolerate intolerable things," he said.

"Are you threatening me?" she said.

Brother Thomas sighed. Then he smiled, but not kindly.

"Fine. Since you just admitted before witnesses to murdering Dean Floden, I'll call the police and tell them. May I borrow your phone?" he said, not at all quietly.

"I did no such thing!" she shrieked.

"I distinctly heard you say that because he discovered that you had been sleeping with one of your students, you murdered him." He said it loudly enough that the people in the next office would probably have heard even if they were hard of hearing.

"What are you doing?" she asked, still angry, but with a note of fear mixed in.

Brother Thomas stared at her for a second.

"Is it that student who just left?"

"Get out of here," Dr. Marten said.

"How long have you been sleeping with him?" Brother Thomas asked, at a volume just under a shout.

Dr. Marten turned pale.

"Get out of here!" she shrieked.

Brother Thomas walked, slowly, to the door. He stopped and turned around when he had crossed it.

"Did you get him to do it for you?" he asked.

"Get out of here!" she screamed even louder.

"I'm already out of your office. Did you get him to murder the dean for you?" he said, calmly, back at a normal volume.

"Leave me alone. Just leave me alone!"

"That's cold," he said.

"Why can't you just leave me alone?" she asked, starting to cry.

"On a serious note, if you have any ideas of killing yourself before the police come to get you, please seek professional help. You can call 911 and they'll happily redirect you. Good day," Brother Thomas said.

He walked off in the direction that the grad student had gone. The others walked out of Dr. Marten's office. Michael, who was the last, turned around as he was leaving.

"He's right. 911 will happily forward you to a suicide prevention hotline," he said.

Brother Thomas was walking briskly. He didn't see the grad student in any of the offices, but they all appeared to belong to professors. There was a stairwell at the end of the hallway, and Brother Thomas went into it and all but ran up the stairs.

He walked with great haste along the corridor. The others got to the top of the stairs in time to see him duck into an office. They caught up with him a few seconds later.

"...important to tell you," he said as they walked in.

"What is that?" the grad student asked. His clean-shaven cheeks seemed a bit tense.

"Look, I'm going to tell you the important thing, without stopping, and you really shouldn't say anything, so please don't bother to deny it. When I get to the end, I'm just going to leave," Brother Thomas said. "Okay?"

"Say what you have to say," the grad student said.

"I was just speaking with Dr. Marten and she admitted to how she seduced you and got you to kill the dean for her."

The grad student turned visibly pale.

"While we don't have all of the evidence to convict you yet, it's really only a matter of time. And something you need to be aware of in the criminal justice system is that when a man and a woman commit a crime together, usually the man takes the blame, and the woman tends to get off. Usually she does her best to bury him, though she tries to keep that fact from him. Women hate conflict. They prefer backstabbing. It's so much less unpleasant," Brother Thomas continued.

The grad student swallowed and looked like he was going to say something.

"Don't tell me anything. I'm not your lawyer, and anything you tell me would help to convict you. I may end up contributing to you going to prison, but I don't want to do that by taking advantage of you trusting me," Brother Thomas said.

The grad student sat stony-faced, possibly taking the advice he was offered.

"What you need to do, without delay, is to find a decent lawyer. They're not cheap, but you're better off going into debt than getting a significantly longer prison sentence than you might otherwise. Do it as soon as you can. And whatever you do, don't go to your accomplice for advice. One of the effects of sin is to separate man from man. You and your accomplice have very different interests, so she's not likely to have your best interests close to her heart. And remember that she is someone whose range of problem-solving techniques includes murder. If murder is thinkable, do you think betraying a lover is unthinkable?"

For whatever reason, good or bad, the grad student didn't react.

"I'm very sorry to be telling you this. It probably looks like I'm trying to divide and conquer, to play one of you off of the other. That's not what I'm doing. She's taking advantage of you, and I dislike seeing people being taken advantage of. That doesn't mean I'll let you get away with anything, if I can help it, but I want you to protect yourself. The legal system can screw people over. Hard," Thomas concluded.

The grad student was quiet for a moment, then very carefully said, "Thank you for your concern."

"God be with you," Thomas said, and left.

Michael was again the last one to leave, and before he did so, he said, "In case you're ever feeling hopeless, you can call 911 and they'll put you in touch with a suicide hotline where someone will listen to your troubles, confidentially."

They walked silently out of the building, and stopped a short distance away.

"What was that?" Sonia asked.

"Clarify?" Brother Thomas said.

"You were really mean to Dr. Marten. I'm not saying that she didn't deserve it, but I don't think I've seen anyone on this campus be half that mean to anyone else," she said.

"She made it very clear that she wasn't going to cooperate at all. It is said, in vino veritas—in wine there is truth—

but there are other things which make people honest. Angry people, for example, are often far more truthful than calm people are," he said.

"Like I said, it's not like she didn't deserve it. It's just weird to see somebody being treated like they deserve around here," she said.

Brother Thomas shrugged his shoulders.

"It can be very liberating to know that you're never going to deal with somebody again. You should always treat people well, of course, but much of what is called politeness is actually being dishonest to people so they're easier to get along with. In the end, it's laziness, more than it is treating people well."

"Do you really think that she did it?" Sonia asked.

"I'm not certain, but I'm more inclined to it than not," Brother Thomas said.

"That seemed pretty ambiguous to me. At best," Sonia said.

"An explicit confession would be clearer, certainly. We need to find evidence to prove it as much to know if it's true as to be able to prove it legally," he said.

"And the stuff you said to the grad student?" Sonia asked.

"His name is Paresh," Brother Thomas said.

"Okay, the stuff that you said to Paresh. How much of that did you mean?" she asked.

Brother Thomas seemed surprised at the question.

"All of it," he said.

"You know, when you found those condoms in Tiffany's drawer, I kind of bought the conclusion that she was sleeping with Jack. I mean, I wasn't sold on it, but at least I understood why you'd think that. But why did you think that Dr. Marten was sleeping with Paresh? As far as I could see, there was no evidence at all of that," Sonia said.

"It was just a shot in the dark. It was her reaction to the accusation which told me," Brother Thomas said.

"So you just got lucky?" she asked.

Brother Francis cut in.

"It's like fishing. It's not enough to go out on the water in a boat. If you put a baited hook into the water, in the right spot, at the right time of day, you might possibly catch something. If you do that and catch something, you were fortunate. Luck is when you were on the lake for a pleasure cruise and the fish jumps into your boat anyway."

Sonia laughed.

"So what's the next step?" she asked.

"Well, we still have several other people to talk to who spoke to the dean on Friday," Brother Thomas said. "After that, we need to run down the physical evidence. And we really need to talk with the police. As suggestive as those hypodermic needles were, we need to make sure that they really were the murder weapons. Not to mention that we need to tell the police about them. Perhaps that should be our first stop. Will you come with us and smile so the sheriff will be friendly?"

"I don't think that you need my help to get along with people," Sonia said.

"Perhaps I don't, but it can be nice to have help even when it's not strictly necessary. Besides, people are always on their best behavior in front of witnesses," he said.

Sonia laughed.

"I wouldn't miss it anyway," she said.

"I think it might be better if I didn't accompany you," Michael said.

"Your lack of presence would be easier to not explain than

your presence would be to explain," Brother Thomas concurred.

"I'll check out the library. It's always quite interesting to look through old collections," Michael said.

"Ours has plenty of old books. Unlike many of the older buildings around here, I don't think that it ever burned down," Sonia said.

Michael smiled, waved, and walked off in the direction of the library. Evidently he had spent a few minutes studying the campus map.

Brother Thomas, Brother Francis, and Sonia walked in the direction of the police station. Nothing around Yalevard was an especially long walk, and they arrived in about twenty minutes. As luck would have it, the sheriff was on his way back in, and they only had to wait about ten minutes for him.

The sheriff was a middle-aged man, though he had not yet reached his fifties. His hair was a medium brown without gray, and if he was solidly built, yet he was far from fat, and had a brisk, energetic manner. Police officers are professionally suspicious, but though this had not faded since his election as sheriff, he managed to put a friendly spin on it. He didn't mind upsetting people, and so he had no need to warn them off of making requests he was going to deny, or trying to ingratiate themselves while doing it.

"Good afternoon," he said, in a noncommittal manner, when the officer at the desk pointed them out.

"May we speak to you in your office, sir?" Brother Thomas asked in a deferential tone.

"Come in," the sheriff said with a friendly wave at one of the open doors.

He led the way through it and sat down behind his desk.

When his three guests sat down, he looked at them expectantly, but didn't commit himself to anything with words.

Deciding to humor Brother Thomas, Sonia smiled, but didn't say anything.

"Our main reason for taking up your time is that we discovered what we believe to be evidence related to the murder of Dean Floden. However, before we get into that, I believe a word of introduction is in order. I am Brother Thomas, and this is Brother Francis. We are members of a small order called the Franciscan Brothers of Investigation. It is an order of consulting detectives, where our mission is to help people by discovering the truth behind mysteries. Since you will no doubt ask, we are licensed private investigators, though we do not in fact charge a fee for our service. President Blendermore, of whom Dr. Olivera here is a representative, has asked us to investigate the death of Dean Floden, which is why we are here."

The sheriff's expression was difficult to read, but Brother Thomas believed that its chief component was amusement.

"So he doesn't have faith that we'll solve the case?" the sheriff asked, with perilous gentleness.

"It is the logical deduction to make, but I am not empowered to speak for the President, nor have I ever read his mind," Brother Thomas said.

"I wouldn't expect you to speak for him, but isn't that what the professor is here for?" the sheriff asked, his tone conveying no particular emotion.

It was clear that everyone was sounding each other out, and trying to give nothing away.

"I'm not a professor, I'm Dr. Blendermore's secretary. I'm just here as a guide, and to make introductions," Sonia said.

"Which you didn't do," the sheriff observed.

"This being outside of the university, it doesn't seem my place to make introductions," she replied.

"I asked her to come along because I had no idea how you would take our presence here, and she has a nicer smile than I do," Brother Thomas said.

The sheriff laughed.

"That shows good sense."

For a few moments he looked at the brothers intently, while no one said anything.

"Have you investigated many murders before?" he asked, clearly not having made up his mind.

"Personally, none. The order has investigated a few within the lifetime of some of the older brothers, and certainly a decent number within its existence. In fact, that was how the order was founded—some French nobleman's wife died under suspicious circumstances, and the bishop who was to remarry him wanted to make sure that the first wife did in fact die of natural causes. Or at least if not, that it was not her husband who killed her. He asked around, and there were some Franciscan brothers who had been police detectives before joining the order, and a formal, if discreet, request was made to the head of the order, and they investigated. Somehow word spread of this capability, and other bishops took advantage of it, until all concerned thought it more sensible to create an order dedicated to the task than to constantly pull the brothers away from their duties."

"Did he do it?" the sheriff asked.

"You mean the nobleman whose wife died under suspicious circumstances?" Brother Thomas asked.

"Yes."

"I'm afraid so."

The sheriff smiled.

"So what do you normally investigate?" he asked.

"Most of our clients come to us over cases of suspected marital infidelity," Brother Thomas said.

"Sounds awful," the sheriff said.

"It can be unpleasant, but it's good work. We don't merely try to discover marital infidelity; we treat it as a symptom, and also try to uncover the root causes, then help people to fix them. Our work is not to destroy marriages, but to repair them," Brother Thomas said.

"What's your success rate?" the sheriff asked.

"Of the people where there is infidelity, ten percent of them split up generally, three percent if they have children," Brother Thomas said.

"That's a lot better than I would have expected," the sheriff said.

Brother Thomas shrugged his shoulders deprecatingly.

"We're trying to improve those rates, especially in the cases with children," he said.

"So how does this make you qualified to investigate murder?" the sheriff asked. It was a genuine question, not a rhetorical one.

"Infidelity is not the only thing we investigate. We've investigated theft, fraud, industrial espionage, sabotage, and even counterfeiting, once. Our experience is that while particular experience is useful, investigation is largely the same regardless of what's being investigated," Brother Thomas said.

"I suppose that's the same reason police departments have general officers and not ten thousand specialists," the sheriff said.

"Indeed," Brother Thomas said.

The sheriff smiled. He seemed to have made a decision.

"Don't worry about what I said earlier about the president

not trusting me. I'm not sure that I would, in his position. And to be perfectly frank, as long as you don't get in my way, I think I'd rather have your help than have the state police come in. I can't tell them to go to hell if I want to."

Brother Thomas smiled.

"So what is it you found?" the sheriff asked.

Brother Thomas told him about the syringe caps and then about the syringes. He pulled out his phone and showed the pictures.

"That's very interesting," the sheriff said.

"We left them where we found them so you can go and discover them yourself," Brother Thomas said.

"You should have called us as soon as you found them. For all we know the murderer has come and retrieved them," the sheriff said.

"I apologize for that. It seems unlikely that someone would wait this long to retrieve something, if he planned to retrieve it, but you're right—we should have notified you earlier. I had no intention of withholding any evidence, it's just that we don't often deal in cases for which criminal prosecution is likely, so documenting the evidence is more important than securing it, by habit. Should we come across anything else, we won't make that mistake again," Brother Thomas said.

"What's done is done. You're probably right that this many days after the murder, the murderer is unlikely to be out and about retrieving things. Still, I'm going to go out there right now to secure the evidence," the sheriff said.

"If you'll forgive me delaying you for a moment, have you released the cause of death?" Brother Thomas asked.

"No. Can you keep a secret?" the sheriff asked.

"Yes," Brother Thomas said.

"So can I," the sheriff said, and laughed at his own joke.

Brother Thomas looked slightly cross.

"I'm just kidding. Don't repeat this to anyone, but he died of a heroin overdose. A massive heroin overdose. Delivered through two injections, one in the neck—on the right side—the other in the vein in his left arm," the sheriff said.

"As you might have seen in the pictures, the syringes were empty, but you can probably find something in the needle itself," Brother Thomas said.

The sheriff nodded and got up. The brothers and Sonia also rose.

"Oh, is it true that the cold let in through the open windows has made establishing a time of death impossible?" Brother Thomas asked.

"As near as makes no difference. He does have to have been killed at least four hours before he was found, but you could tell that just by looking at him. Plus, the dean never came in early, so the first person in the building finding him rules it out," the sheriff said.

"Thank you. If we find anything else, the first thing we'll do is let you know," Brother Thomas said.

"Thank you. And good luck," the sheriff said.

As they were walking out of the police station, the sheriff called out to them.

"By the way, my name's Greg."

Brother Thomas turned, smiled, and waved goodbye.

They walked back to the campus, and paused to decide where they would go when they got to the main crossroads.

"I think we should look up Mr. Blakely," Brother Thomas said.

"Who?" Sonia asked.

"The dean's marijuana supplier," Brother Thomas said.

"I can look him up in the campus directory. It's not publicly available for anything but professor's offices," Sonia said.

Brother Thomas nodded.

Sonia pulled out her phone and began typing. She was not nearly as adept as Brother Thomas at searching for things on her phone, and they stood for a minute or so before Sonia announced that she had his address.

"I've texted Michael about what we're going to do, but he's found an old translation of St. Augustine's confessions, so he would prefer to stay in the library for now," Brother Thomas said.

"Why would he be so interested in an old translation?" Sonia asked.

"Partially out of historical curiosity, and partially because early translations were a bit closer to ancient usage than modern translations, and partially because they were more steeped in Latin as a living language. Of course, he also likes to see how other people translated things," Brother Thomas said.

"What, has he published a translation of the Confessions?" Sonia asked.

"Yes, though not commercially. He gives it away for free," Brother Thomas said.

"He really doesn't look like what you'd expect a classics scholar to look like," Sonia said.

"Do you look like what anyone else would expect a differential geometer to look like?" Brother Thomas asked.

Sonia blushed slightly.

"As it happens, Michael is an expert in Greek and Latin, and reasonably fluent in written Chinese," Brother Thomas said.

"And yet he's a kung fu teacher?" Sonia asked.

"One has to pay the bills somehow. Besides, he's also quite devoted to being a kung fu master. Hung Gar, specifically. When you have several loves, it makes sense to do the most lucrative one professionally," Brother Thomas said.

"I suppose it does," Sonia said.

They walked on, and came to the apartment building in which Jordan Blakely lived. In truth, it was an old Victorian house which had been repurposed to be an apartment building. They knocked on the door, and a tall young woman in sweatpants and a sweater opened it.

"Hello," she said, eying the religious habits suspiciously, probably afraid she might be asked if she loved Jesus.

"We're looking for Jordan," Sonia said.

"I'm Jordan," she said.

"Blakely?" Sonia asked, confused.

"Oh! He's in his room, I think. I'll go get him for you," the young woman said, giggling.

She closed the door and they could hear her walking towards the center of the house and shouting, "Jordan!"

"She could have invited us in rather than leaving us out in the cold," Sonia said.

"Alas, detecting is not always comfortable," said Brother Thomas.

He moved to be shoulder to shoulder with Brother Francis, forming a windbreak upwind of Sonia.

"Thanks," she said.

"I'm originally from Michigan, so I don't mind the cold, or at least not the cold that you find around here," Brother Francis said. And indeed, Sonia noticed, his coat was not zipped all the way up.

"I find two layers of thick wool to be equal to any winter I've come across yet," Brother Thomas said.

"This coat is thick goose down, and I'm still cold," Sonia said.

"Do you want me to deduce that you're from a warm climate again? I'll grant you that in this weather it is preferable to juggling," Brother Thomas said.

Sonia gave him a dirty look, which he ignored.

Presently they heard footsteps coming to the door, and an unkempt, dirty-sweatshirt-wearing young man, who might as well have been trying to fulfill the stereotype of a college student pot dealer, opened it.

"Hi," he said.

"May we come in? Our friend finds the weather a bit chilly for her taste," Brother Thomas said.

"Whatever," Jordan said. He had a hint of a European accent that might have been French.

Sonia, who was cold, disregarded the fact that he didn't move after the invitation and walked past him into the house. The brothers followed, though by this time Jordan had moved a little in order to avoid being bumped into. Brother Francis closed the door behind him.

"So what do you want?" Jordan asked.

"What do you have?" Brother Thomas asked.

"What do you mean by that?" Jordan asked.

"I mean, what do you have to offer us," Brother Thomas said.

"I don't know you," Jordan said.

"We're not police, but we are detectives. We don't care what illegal substances you're selling, but we know that you supplied the late Dean Jack Floden with marijuana—or do you prefer the term weed?" Brother Thomas asked.

"I don't care," Jordan said.

"No, of course you don't," Brother Thomas said.

He paused for a second.

"So we know that you sold him some sort of THC-laden consumable-"

"Did he prefer leaf or brownies?" Brother Francis cut in.

"Brownies," Jordan said.

"-and that you visited him at his office last Friday," Brother Thomas concluded.

"Yeah," Jordan said, and nodded very slightly.

"Was it to make a delivery?" Brother Thomas asked.

"Yeah," Jordan said.

"Did Floden pay in cash?"

"Well, yeah. It's not like I take credit cards. It would be kind of cool if I could, though. I heard from a buddy that there's a way to take credit cards with an iPhone. I should look into that," Jordan said.

"Indeed you should. Did he have the money readily available? As opposed to stalling, or saying that he would pay you later?" Brother Thomas asked.

"Dude, I'm not a bank. I've gotten into too many problems letting people pay me back later. Then you have to keep after them, and I don't like remembering to pay my own bills. Just ask my roommates," Jordan said.

"I know that remembering specifics can be difficult, especially while high, but do you recall what mood Dean Floden was in? Did he seem happy, anxious, afraid, or anything unusual?"

"I don't remember him being any different. He was, you know, chill enough. He was never what you would call mellow. He had a stressful job. That's why he bought so much. I never really talked with him. I mean, the dude was like sixty or something, and had no taste in music. He let me drop a class after the deadline once. That was pretty cool," Jordan

said.

"It sounds very... cool," Brother Thomas agreed.

Jordan nodded.

"Do you recall how many arms Dean Floden had that day?" Brother Thomas asked.

"Arms? Two. He always had two," Jordan said.

"He sounds very conventional," Brother Thomas said.

"Well, I mean, you know, he was a dean. You have to be. I mean, to be a Dean," Jordan said.

"Very true. Was there anything at all unusual about that day, or was everything normal?" Brother Thomas asked.

"I don't know, man," Jordan said. He rubbed his head in thought.

"Actually, you know, there was this one dude who came in when I was leaving. I had gotten a text and sat down to answer it, and I guess I got a little distracted, and like a minute later he came in. He, like, didn't see me, and he was looking into the empty offices, and when I stood up, he jumped like he saw a ghost. Then he went into the bathroom. That was weird, cause I mean, who's afraid of me?"

It started as a rhetorical question, but seemed in Jordan's mind to have turned into a real question, because he waited for a reply.

"Probably very few people. Possibly your parents. Did you notice anything else about this guy who acted weird? How old was he? What did he look like?" Brother Thomas asked.

"He was older than me, but I don't think he was a professor. He wasn't real tall. He wasn't fat. Oh, yeah, he was Indian. You know, like 7-11 Indian," Jordan said.

"I'm guessing that your parents are afraid of you, in the sense of being afraid of what you're doing to their child,"

Brother Thomas said.

"Did he ever buy anything heavier than pot? Like coke or heroin?" Brother Francis broke in.

"I don't know, man. I only sell pot, so he wouldn't have told me," Jordan said.

"Still, if he wanted it, he might have asked you if you sold it," Brother Francis pointed out.

"I don't think he ever did," Jordan said.

"Supposing he did want any, do you know who he should have asked?" Brother Francis persisted.

Jordan looked from Brother Francis to Brother Thomas and back.

"Nah, man," he said.

"Don't worry, we won't tell him where we heard his name from, and he won't figure it out for himself: drug dealers are pretty stupid," Brother Thomas said.

"Well, that's true. I don't know. You promise that you didn't hear it from me?" Jordan asked.

"We promise," Brother Thomas said.

"Jordan," he said in a low voice, and nodded his head in the direction of where she was sitting on a couch, absorbed in her phone.

Brother Thomas did not, as a rule, have a high opinion of either drug users or drug dealers, mostly as a result of his experience with them. His expectations for the young man he was interviewing were, therefore, not very high. Nonetheless, he stood there stunned for a few moments.

He opened his mouth to say something, then closed it again. He thought furiously for a way to keep the implied promise to the one Jordan while still asking the other Jordan for the information they wanted. And that, of course, on the strained assumption that she hadn't heard their conversation.

Their conversation which had taken place in the same room as she was and, until the last sentence, not quiet. Usually quick witted, especially in stressful circumstances, he drew a blank this time.

It was Sonia who ended up thinking of something. She walked over to the couch where the female Jordan was sitting and said hello. This Jordan was also dressed in sweatpants and a sweatshirt, but they were fashionable sweats, unlike the male Jordan's ratty and not recently washed clothes. She was thin, though not athletic. She had well tended eyebrows and straight, dirty blond hair with brown roots tied up in a careless ponytail. She wore a few rings on her fingers with no precious stones in them and smelled faintly of perfume. She was pretty enough to manipulate at least weak-willed men.

"Hi," Jordan said, without looking up from her phone.

"Jordan isn't very bright, is he?" Sonia said.

"No," the female Jordan agreed.

"Aren't you worried about having a dumb drug dealer for a roommate?" Sonia asked.

"No," she said.

"But what if the cops find him and raid the house?" Sonia asked.

"If they raided the house, they would discover that Jordan dealt more than just pot," she said.

"I see why you're not worried," Sonia said.

Jordan looked up, without smiling, and said, "What do you want?"

Her tone was a study in neutrality, neither friendly nor impatient.

"We just want to know if Dean Floden was doing any drugs other than marijuana," Sonia said.

Jordan looked at her, considering.

"You're very pretty," she said.

"Thank you," Sonia said.

"My feminine intuition tells me that Dean Floden didn't do anything heavier than weed," Jordan said.

Sonia was about to get up, then paused.

"Would you have told me if he did?" she asked.

The female Jordan considered that.

"Maybe. It's not nice to speak ill of the dead. On the other hand, I'm not nice," she said.

Sonia was confused. On the one hand she instinctively liked this Jordan, but on the other, she scared her.

"You're playing a dangerous game, aren't you?" Sonia asked.

"I don't intend to play it forever. After college, I plan to marry and settle down," Jordan said.

"I don't think you'll have any problems with that. You're quite pretty yourself," Sonia said.

"Thanks. The difference is that I have to work at it. Good luck with your investigation," Jordan said, and went back to her phone.

Sonia got up, unsure of what to make of her conversation. She decided to just relate the whole thing to the brothers and see what they made of it. She walked back to them. They had ostensibly been talking with Jordan, but had really just been waiting for her.

"God be with you," Brother Thomas abruptly said to the male Jordan, and walked out with Sonia.

When they were outside, Brother Thomas waited only a few moments before exclaiming, "I have met some dumb people in my time, but I think this is a record!"

"It was all I could do to keep from laughing when he told us Jordan was the drug dealer. Not only did your joke about drug dealers being stupid fly over his head, he went and proved it! Do you think it's the marijuana? He couldn't possibly be that dumb natively, could he?" Brother Francis said.

"I think it likely. People high on marijuana are especially dumb, but the effect lasts for some time afterwards and there is clinical research to back up the effects being long-term cumulative. I really don't understand what the attraction of performing a temporary chemical lobotomy on yourself is, especially if it's not entirely temporary," Brother Thomas said.

"I also nearly lost it when you asked him how many arms Dean Floden had. And then he explained why the dean was so conventional about the number of arms he had!" Brother Francis said, laughing at the recollection.

"I originally meant it to double-check Jordan's memory, rather than as humor, but couldn't resist when the opportunity presented itself. Anyway, how did your conversation with the other Jordan go, Sonia? Was she brighter than the marijuana dealer in the house bearing that name? She looked it, when she answered the door," Brother Thomas asked.

"She's a lot smarter," Sonia said.

She recounted the conversation, as close to verbatim as she could. At first she was going to leave the part out where Jordan complimented her beauty, but decided to include it as the sort of thing that would interest Brother Francis, if not Brother Thomas.

"That's what I expected, but I do wonder if she can be trusted," Brother Thomas said when she had finished.

"I think so, though I can't give you any reasons to back that up," Sonia said.

"What she said has the ring of truth to it. And while drug dealers do not always hold honesty to be the most important virtue, she had no reason to lie to us," Brother Francis said.

"If she sells heroin, then in a town this small there's a decent chance that she sold the murderer the murder weapon. Or at least the lethal part of the murder weapon, if the needles came from somewhere else," Brother Thomas said.

They thought on that for a moment.

"Wouldn't her best interest be to suggest that he died of suicide, rather than murder?" Brother Francis asked.

"If suicide were a maintainable theory, I suppose so," Brother Thomas said.

"It's not that unmaintainable; he could have injected himself—granted, in the neck is unlikely—and then threw the needles out the window for some reason. Heroin addicts don't always have a good reason for everything that they do. And unless Jordan was actually the murderer, she wouldn't know most of the details since they haven't been made public. She has no way of knowing that suicide or accident was especially unlikely," Brother Francis said.

"But if she were the murderer, which is the case in which she would most need to deceive us, she would know suicide to be implausible. In which case, attempting to divert suspicion would itself be suspicious," Brother Thomas said.

"And yet the circumstances of the crime scene were, presumably, under the murderer's control," said Brother Francis.

"That's true," Brother Thomas said.

"What do you mean?" Sonia asked.

"Just that the murderer could have left the needles in the room, and generally staged things to suggest suicide rather than to contradict it," Brother Francis said.

"So what does that tell you about Jordan?" Sonia asked.

"Nothing. Not all speculation leads somewhere. Sometimes you must follow a line of thought just to know that it doesn't lead anywhere," Brother Thomas said.

Sonia smiled.

"So what do you make of the guy who Jordan—pot dealer Jordan—saw acting strangely?" Brother Francis asked.

"It certainly could be Paresh," Brother Thomas said.

"Acting suspiciously in the office of the deceased on the last day he was seen alive doesn't look good for him, if it was Paresh," Brother Francis said.

"It doesn't, though we know that the dean made it home alive. If he waited there to ambush Dean Floden, he waited an awfully long time, and had some reason to suspect that the Dean would come back," Brother Thomas said.

"Don't you think we should make sure that it was Paresh?" Sonia asked.

"I'm fairly certain that it was Paresh, and I really don't feel like talking to Jordan again. 7-11 Indians! And I'll give you one hundred-to-one that he's a liberal and thinks that racism is a conservative trait!"

"I'll do it for you. Potheads don't bother me as much," Brother Francis said.

"Thanks," Brother Thomas said, and handed Brother Francis his phone with a picture of Paresh on it. Brother Francis never ceased to be amazed how quickly Brother Thomas could search for things on his phone without ever obviously looking at it.

Brother Francis walked back to the house, knocked on the door, and spoke to the male Jordan, who answered it this time. It took a few moments to get the answer he was looking for, then he thanked Jordan again and returned to Brother Thomas and Sonia.

"He appeared quite confident that the person he saw acting strangely was the person in the picture," Brother Francis

said.

"Of course, witness identification of people they don't know is notoriously unreliable," Brother Thomas said.

"True," Brother Francis said.

"And potheads don't always make the most reliable witnesses either," Brother Thomas added.

"Also true," Brother Francis said cheerfully.

"On the other hand, we have good reason to believe that he was right, considering how guilty Paresh and Dr. Marten acted," Brother Thomas said.

"What would Paresh have to do with it? I mean, I get that Dr. Marten and Dean Floden had a fight, but why would Paresh go and kill him?" Sonia asked.

"You may have noticed that Dr. Marten is emotionally manipulative, and eager to deflect responsibility," Brother Thomas said.

"Yes," Sonia said.

"She would not be the first woman to convince a man to do her dirty work for her," Brother Thomas said.

"But to get him to murder someone for her?" Sonia said, incredulously.

"If it happened, she would hardly be the first," Brother Thomas said. "Some women, like some men, don't like to take responsibility for their actions. It's made easier for the women by the fact that most men have an almost pathological desire to please women."

"To *please* women?" Sonia asked.

"It's been described rather coarsely as an attempt to obtain sex, but it's far more a desire for approval than it is for the sex act itself. Sex simply happens to be the greatest form of approval it is possible to bestow. What higher compliment can a woman pay a man than to say that she wants to have his children?"

"Good job?" Sonia suggested. "Women have sex for a lot of reasons besides to have children, including just wanting to have sex."

"I will grant you that contraceptives lessen the compliment significantly, were anyone to think about it. Fortunately for the manipulators of the world, no one thinks about anything. That's left to a few weirdos like me who get told that we think too much. But in fact you are right, there are other ways for a woman to grant approval besides sex, I was just explaining the sexual angle."

"I'm glad you think that women are more than just a pair of legs," Sonia said, as much teasing as seriously.

"That's an interesting choice of phrase," said Brother Thomas. "It was said that Helen of Troy's face launched a thousand ships. That may be better put than the original poet knows: beauty is pleasant to look at, but men rarely die for beauty. There's too much beauty all around to make *one* beautiful thing worth dying for. There's always a sunset or a tree or a rose to look at. But a face can smile at you. It's not the smile that matters, it's the *at you*. All faces look like the face of God to us, but the prettier the face, the easier it is to mistake for the original, as I was reminded recently. Is there anything anyone would not do to see the face of God smiling at him?"

He stared at her, waiting for an answer with all the concentration of a tiger about to pounce. It scared Sonia, even though she knew it was harmless.

"Do you really think that she got him to murder the dean for her?" she asked in a hushed voice.

Brother Thomas seemed to relax, though in fact his attention had shifted back to the case.

"It's looking increasingly like it. There are still things that don't fit, however, and we need to either reconcile them or prove Paresh innocent," he said.

"One thing that bothers me is that Paresh didn't seem hardy enough to attack a man directly, at least in cold blood," Brother Francis said.

"It's not like the dean was beaten to death," Brother Thomas said.

"Yes," said a deep voice from the woods next to where they were standing, "But people generally don't stand still while you inject them in the neck."

They all turned to see Michael walking out from behind a tree.

"How long have you been there!" Sonia asked, in a voice closer to a shriek than she had intended.

"Just a moment. I finished looking through the sections of the book I was especially interested in, and came to join you," Michael said.

"How did you know where we were?" Sonia demanded.

"I texted him where we'd be," Brother Thomas said.

"Why did you sneak up on us like that?" Sonia asked, still on edge.

"I didn't. I took a shortcut down the hill to get here, and it's my habit when walking through the woods to be quiet. As I mentioned, I'm a bowhunter, and you have to get close to the animals with a bow. If you never let yourself clomp through the woods, you won't accidentally start just because you've gotten tired or are thinking about a line from Aristotle," Michael said.

"We're not deer," Sonia said.

"I wasn't stalking you. You were just paying less attention to your surroundings than you realized," he said.

"Next time, wave or something?" Sonia said.

"I actually did, but none of you were looking in this direction. But on the subject we were discussing earlier, Francis is right. Injecting somebody with something against their will is not for the faint of heart. It's pretty easy to struggle enough to get a needle out of you, and injections are not instant. The murderer would have needed to hold Dean Floden down, at least during the first injection," Michael said.

"And while I grant you that Paresh might murder for Dr. Marten, I don't think that he would turn physically courageous for her," Brother Francis said.

"Physical courage is usually achieved through training, anger, defensive fear, or drugs," Michael said.

"Except for possibly the last one, which we just have no evidence for, none of those would apply to Paresh. Do you think he hid out in the bathroom for hours until Dean Floden came back to Marduk Hall for some inexplicable reason, then took some—what drug would he take?" Brother Francis asked.

"There's nothing that's reliable for everyone, and it's more likely a matter of what he found while Googling than what would be effective anyway. He would be most likely to try stimulants like amphetamines or cocaine. You'd have to be insane to try things that would calm you down before grappling with a person for your life. If it was cold blooded murder, I don't think you'd want to try inducing a berserker rage with hallucinogens. You'd certainly leave evidence that way," Michael said.

"Thanks," Brother Francis said. "So do you see Paresh waiting in the bathroom for hours hopped up on cocaine and amphetamines, a syringe full of heroin clutched in each hand?"

"While it is an amusing image to contemplate, I must confess it seems unlikely," Brother Thomas said. "But if Paresh wasn't there to ambush Dean Floden, what was he there for?"

"Wasn't there a mini-fridge in the dean's office?" Brother Francis asked.

"There was, against the exterior wall, to the left as you faced his desk. It was running," Brother Thomas replied.

"Where there is a refrigerator, there is usually food," Brother Francis said.

"I can't believe that we didn't look inside it. Sonia, do you still have the keys to the office?" Brother Thomas said.

"Yes," she said, and held them up.

They walked, briskly, in the direction of Marduk Hall.

It was getting late in the day, and the street lights had come on by the time they got there. Sonia opened the front door. After carefully wiping their feet—if they had missed one clue, perhaps there was another, and why contaminate the crime scene?—they went up to the dean's office. The door was still locked, as it should have been. Sonia unlocked it, and they went in, Brother Thomas leading the way.

They went into the dean's office, turned on the light, and went straight to the mini fridge. It was humming quietly. Brother Thomas opened it gingerly, avoiding all of the main surfaces.

"Do you really think that there could be fingerprints?" Michael asked.

"No, but if he hasn't already, I think that the sheriff will want to dust for them. If he finds none, or finds them all smudged, he's going to ask me if I touched it. While it's not a crime for me to do so since the police have left and the crime scene tape is down, I'd rather not take the risk of getting on his bad side. He's cautiously friendly and I don't want to give him reason to regret that," Brother Thomas said.

The fridge was not well-stocked. It had a few cold cuts in sealed plastic, a package of American cheese, a few sodas, and a bottle of rum.

"Is it normal to keep rum in a refrigerator?" Brother Francis asked.

"It's not common, but neither is it weird. Some people like their hard liquor cold, especially if it is going to be mixed with something else, like for example the Coca Cola that's here," Brother Thomas said.

"I suppose it also has the advantage of being less obvious than if it were out on the shelf," Brother Francis said.

"You can't easily get ice cubes into a can of coke, which presumably he used for rum-and-coke in order to be discrete in case someone important came in," Michael said.

"At this point, I wouldn't be surprised if it turned out that the reason the windows were open was because the dean was smoking a joint and didn't want the smell of the smoke to linger in his office," Brother Thomas said.

"How on earth did this man ever become a dean?" Sonia asked.

"It's not that difficult for people to show only the sides of themselves that others want to see," Brother Thomas said.

"And people change. Who knows whether he had these habits before he became Dean?" Michael added.

"And while Brother Thomas is correct that marijuana has the effect of a temporary chemical lobotomy, it also tends to make people more relaxed and less aggressive. Which a lobotomy also does, I suppose. So it's possible that Floden recognized that his dislike of fields other than science was hurting people and he was self-medicating," Brother Francis

said.

Brother Thomas had been inspecting the contents of the refrigerator carefully during this discussion.

"The meat and cheese are both unopened in sealed plastic whose vacuum appears to be intact, so I doubt that they have been poisoned," he said.

He examined the cans of soda and replaced them. Then he picked up the bottle of rum.

"This appears to have little pieces of something in the bottom of it," he said.

He looked around the office. "Do we have anything long? A bamboo skewer would be ideal, but I think that's too much to ask for. Could someone find a paperclip for me?"

Sonia went to Tiffany's desk, opened the top drawer, and got a paperclip. She unbent and straightened it as she brought it to Brother Thomas, who was holding the bottle of rum upside down. He propped it on the floor against the refrigerator to hold it in that position and took the paperclip, straightened it further, then bent the end into a hook.

He picked up the bottle of rum and very slowly turned it sideways, so that the small pieces remained in the neck, unscrewed the cap, and used the paperclip to fish one of the pieces out. He replaced the cap and put the bottle back into the refrigerator.

He put the particle on the window sill and poked at it. It was firm, but not hard, almost like rubber. He looked at it intently, then sniffed it.

"Michael, what do you think this is?"

Michael repeated the inspection, then sniffed it a few times.

"I'm not sure," he said.

He nudged the mystery substance along, then took a tissue out of his pocked and blotted it dry. He then opened the refrigerator and took out the bottle of rum. He opened it and held it under his nose, sniffing it for the better part of a minute.

"Hopefully the stuff, if it has a smell, didn't impart too much into the rum," he said.

"Are you numbing your nose to the smell of the rum so you can pick up whatever's in the crumb?" Sonia asked.

"I'm trying it out," Michael said.

He then put the bottle down, took a pocket knife out of his pocket, and cut the particle in half. He sniffed it again.

"I can't be sure, but I think that's rat bait," he said.

"I couldn't smell anything over the rum, but that was my guess," Brother Thomas said.

"Isn't rat poison supposed to be odorless and tasteless?" Brother Francis asked.

"The poison itself, yes," Michael said.

"But not the stuff they mix it with?" Sonia asked.

"Rats are not much in the habit of eating odorless and tasteless substances. Food generally has a flavor. Also, how would they ever find it except if it smelled like something?" Michael said.

"So how did it get in here?" Sonia asked.

"I believe we've discovered what Paresh was doing in the building," Brother Thomas said.

"It would fit far better than sitting for hours in the bathroom, hopped up on cocaine and amphetamines, with a syringe full of heroin clutched in each hand. Just waiting patiently in case the dean happened to come back to his office in the middle of a blizzard," Brother Francis said.

"But the dean did come back to his office in the middle of a blizzard," Sonia said.

"Technically, we don't know that," Brother Thomas pointed out.

"I thought that you said the body wasn't moved," Sonia said.

"I just meant that he could have come back after the blizzard and been killed then."

"So why did Paresh hide in the bathroom?" Sonia asked. She had guessed, but wanted to see how they would say it.

"I think that he went there to wait for everyone to leave," Brother Thomas said. "The cleaning person must have come in, and so he hid in the stall, standing on the toilet. That would explain the footprints we found on the toilet seat. After the cleaning person left, he went upstairs and into Dean Floden's office."

"Wouldn't it have been locked? You said that it didn't look forced," Sonia said.

"Yes, but it's an ancient lock, and should be fairly easy to open with a credit card. Anyone who's watched TV or movies would likely know that trick, despite it not having worked in the last forty years. Unfortunately for Paresh, this lock wasn't made in the last forty years," Brother Thomas said.

"Why unfortunately? Wouldn't that trick working mean that Paresh could get in?" Sonia asked.

"Murder is evil, so any circumstance which helps you to succeed at it is not your friend," Brother Thomas said.

"Do you think that he succeeded?" Sonia asked.

"I don't mean, 'Did he succeed in killing the dean?' since we know the dean died of a heroin overdose, but do you think he was actually poisoned too?" she added.

"I doubt it. Unless the dean had a habit of pouring his rum in the dark after rubbing his mouth down with lidocaine, there's no way he could have accidentally ingested these pieces," Brother Thomas said.

"Then why did they put them in his rum? As a warning?" Sonia asked.

"I doubt that they had any experience with poisoning people," Brother Francis said.

"Or with rat poison. Being water resistant is one of the selling points of rat bait, since bait that dissolves when wet won't kill any rats after it rains," Michael said.

"I've read that poisoning attempts are often unsuccessful simply because poisoning people is not as easy as it seems. Most substances that can kill with trace amounts are hard to get ahold of. Moreover, our digestive systems are fairly good at noticing when there's something dangerous in them and expelling it out of one end or the other before it can do much damage. Obviously people do die from poisoning, but healthy people are hardier than the general public expects," Brother Thomas said.

"So Dr. Marten did get Paresh to kill Dean Floden for her. He was just no good at it," Sonia said.

"I doubt that she would have been any better," Brother Thomas said.

"Poor Jack. Two people tried to kill him on the same day," Sonia said.

Brother Thomas shrugged.

"Sometimes when it rains, it pours. Given what he was like, it wouldn't shock me if we discovered a third attempt on his life before this investigation is over."

"Does this mean that we can rule out Paresh and Dr. Marten?" Sonia asked.

"I think that it does. No one would provide an alibi for themselves murdering somebody by pretending to murder that same person. Not even someone crazy enough to ask me if I thought that she murdered that person because she was a woman," Brother Thomas said.

"Perhaps she's crazy like a fox," Sonia suggested.

"If so, she's crazy like a fox with rabies," Brother Thomas said.

"So what do we do now?" Sonia asked.

"Check out the lead which Tiffany texted me while we were investigating the fridge," Brother Thomas said.

"She remembered something?" Sonia asked.

"She did. Dr. Sarah Gallager stopped by to see Dean Floden in the afternoon while the dean was meeting with the provost. She waited for a few minutes, but left before the dean returned," Brother Thomas said.

"That doesn't sound like much of a lead," Sonia said.

"Important-seeming leads often lead nowhere, and insignificant-seeming leads sometimes turn out to be important. You can't tell before you check them out," Brother Thomas said.

"Do you know what department she's in?" Sonia asked.

"Philosophy, though at this time of day, I doubt that she'd be in her office. Can you look up her home address?" Thomas asked.

Sonia pulled out her phone and found the address.

"What do we do with this stuff?" Brother Francis asked, gesturing at the evidence.

"Let's put it back. Paresh is unlikely to come back for it, and it wouldn't much matter if he did, but let's take our sample with us," Thomas said.

He pulled out a small ziplock bag and picked up the pieces of rat bait with it, then sealed it and put it in his pocket.

"And let's check the bathroom for lurkers before we leave,"

Brother Thomas added, smiling.

The bathroom was empty, and Sonia was careful to lock the front door when they left.

* * *

Dr. Gallager's house was about the same distance away that everything else around the campus seemed to be—about a twenty-minute walk. It was a large Victorian house, painted an attractive navy blue with white trim.

Sonia knocked on the door, and a boy answered it.

"Mom! It's a woman, a big man, and some monks!" he shouted.

A pleasant looking woman in her mid forties came to the door. Her hair was curly brown and neatly groomed, and though she wore no jewelry, she probably owned some. She was healthily thin, of average height, and had a sharp, intelligent look in her eye that did not miss much.

"Actually, Caleb, they're Franciscan friars, not monks," she called to the child who had left when she approached. Turning to the people on her doorstep, she added, "Please pardon my son, he's only eight. And please come in out of the cold."

She held the door wide open, and they came in. Once inside, she shut the door against the night and turned to her guests.

"To what do I owe this pleasure?" she asked.

"My name is Sonia, and I'm acting on behalf of President Blendermore. This is Brother Thomas and Brother Francis, and their associate, Michael."

Hands were shaken.

"They are looking into the death of Dean Floden on behalf of the university," Sonia said.

Brother Thomas produced one of his cards and handed it to Dr. Gallager.

"The Franciscan Brothers of Investigation? The story of the founding of your order must be very interesting. But what can I do for you?" she asked, still smiling.

"We're talking to everybody who was in Dean Floden's office on Friday," Brother Thomas said.

"Oh, I see. I don't have much to tell. I stopped by to talk with him about a tenure vote that will be coming up at the end of next semester. He was not, as a rule, fond of granting anyone tenure who wasn't a scientist, and so I wanted to start laying the groundwork for making the candidate palatable. However, he wasn't there. I waited for a few minutes, maybe twenty, and then I left, since it would seem too eager if I waited a long time," she said.

"Do you remember about what time this was?" Brother Thomas asked.

"It was after I had lunch, so around one o'clock. I wasn't paying close attention to the time," she said.

"Do you have any idea whether Dean Floden had any enemies?" Brother Thomas asked.

Dr. Gallager laughed.

"Whatever fraction of the college of Liberal Arts and Sciences that wasn't a STEM field, plus theoretical physics and math except for cryptography and financial math," she said.

Brother Thomas smiled. He liked candor.

"That's a pretty wide field," he said.

"There were a few of us who figured out how to deal with him. He liked to think of himself as a practical man, which is ironic given how unhappy he was," she said.

"Pardon me, but how is that ironic?" Sonia asked.

"As Aristotle observed in the first sentence of the Metaphysics, all men desire to be happy. To not be happy is to not achieve your goals. And since, as Hamlet observed, nothing is good or bad but thinking makes it so, if you're not happy, it's because you've let some ideal ruin things for you. I don't mean that it's necessarily a stated ideal. In Jack's case it was that he wanted to measure all things against a Materialist standard from the 1800s which no one ever successfully articulated. Measuring with an unfinished yardstick is doomed to failure. Snatching the yardstick up before it's finished and saying that you're not going to wait for it to be done before you start using it because you're too practical is... impractical."

"How did you deal with him?" Brother Francis asked.

"The trick was to express everything in terms of the ideal of Progress that Jack was so fond of. In that sense, it was helpful that it was an unarticulated measure. That made it easier to only consider whatever contradictory part of it was helpful," Dr. Gallager said.

"And that worked?" Brother Francis asked.

"Reasonably well. I think that Jack knew you were gaming him, but I think he appreciated being understood well enough to be gamed. Most people didn't get him even that well, and I think it made him lonely," she said.

"Pragmatists usually are. Most people care more about ideals than results. And they're right," Michael said.

"Idealism is only considering things in their practical essence?" she asked.

"Idealism means that we should first consider a poker in reference to poking, before we consider its suitability for wife beating," Michael answered.

They were both quoting from G.K. Chesterton's book,

What's Wrong With the World, but left it as a private joke and didn't explain the reference.

"Thoroughly worldly people never understand even the world. They rely altogether on a few cynical maxims which are not true," she quoted, this time from G.K.'s masterpiece, *Orthodoxy*.

"It sounds like that might have been a portrait of Dean Floden," Michael said.

Dr. Gallager laughed.

"A hundred years too early, but otherwise, it might have been. Though there was a side to him that would at least commonly be called idealistic. He believed in the singularity," she said.

Michael chuckled, and even Brother Thomas smiled.

"What's the singularity?" Sonia asked.

She was out of her field, and had enough confidence to be willing to admit it publicly.

"It's commonly defined as the point in history, yet to come, when technology will start to create itself. When that happens the rate of technological progress will increase exponentially, AIs using their super-intelligence to develop AIs yet more super intelligent, with each leap being larger and faster than the last," Dr. Gallager said.

Michael cut in.

"If you think of it as, 'And the Word will become silicon, and will dwell among us", you won't go far wrong, especially if you think of the silicon messiah in first century Judaic terms, rather than Christian terms. The singularity isn't supposed to die for our sins, it's supposed to defeat all of our foes and set us up as a nation to rule all other nations, so that all the peoples of the world will know that we're the chosen people of Technology."

"In fairness to your analogy before you clarified it," Brother Thomas interjected, "I believe that the singularity is supposed to conquer death."

Michael laughed.

"I haven't heard that one," Dr. Gallager said.

"It's called 'escape velocity'," Michael explained. "The idea is that life extensions don't need to be infinite in themselves if there can be infinitely many of them. Each one only needs to last until the next life extension is developed, which can be assured because the super-intelligence of the singularity will be growing faster than the problems become difficult. And so there will be a last generation to die, after which everyone will live forever."

"Until they get bored and kill themselves for the fun of it," Dr. Gallager said.

"Well, yes, of course. But no one likes to talk about that part," Michael said.

* * *

The conversation continued in this fashion for over an hour. Most of the talking was done by Dr. Gallager and Michael, who turned out to have a large number of interests, as well as books read, in common. However, they were both polite, and moreover none of the brothers or Sonia were timid, so the conversation was lively and enjoyed by all.

The conversation was interrupted when Dr. Gallager's husband, who had been woodworking in a large, insulated shed in their backyard which served as his workshop, came inside. He was a professor of mathematics, and it turned out that Sonia had met him while she was working on her doctorate. His last name was Varennikov, which is why Sonia didn't recognize the connection. He was thoroughly American, but retained just enough of his Russian heritage to have encouraged his wife to keep her family name when they married. Sonia's field was differential geometry and his was probability, so while they didn't study the same things they had some foundational topics in common.

"I don't know about you guys, but I'm starving. I've been having a great time, but I need to go get something to eat before I pass out," Sonia said.

"Would you like to stay for dinner? I was going to make pizza, and it would be easy to make a second pie," Dr. Gallager said.

She looked at Michael.

"Or two," she added.

"Are you sure?" Sonia asked.

"We wouldn't want to put you to any trouble," Brother Thomas said.

"If you avoid all trouble in life you'll just avoid living," Dr. Gallager said.

"Sarah's pizza is amazing. She says that it's the pizza stone, but I think it's the homemade sauce and mozzarella," Dr. Varennikov said.

"For Brother Francis and myself, we accept," Brother Thomas said.

"It sounds delicious, thank you," Michael said.

Sonia smiled.

"Count me in!" she said.

"If you guys don't mind moving to the kitchen, I'll get started now. Would anyone like a snack while you wait? I have some summer sausage and cheese which goes very well with cold weather like this," Sarah said.

"My name's Peter, and let me take your coats," Dr. Varennikov said.

When the coat-taking had been completed, they followed Sarah into the kitchen, which was large, well furnished, and tastefully decorated. Judging from the large number of tools and machines sensibly arranged, also frequently used.

"So how is the investigation going so far?" Sarah inquired.

Brother Thomas paused awkwardly, which was unusual for him, so Sonia answered instead.

"It's been very eye-opening," she said.

"I can imagine. Bismarck said that people should not learn how laws or sausages are made. And there was someone who, making reference to the Catholic Church, said that those who love the barque of Peter should not go into the engine room," Sarah said.

"That was Cardinal Newman," Michael said.

"You meet that sentiment all over the place. If you like the good that something does, don't find out how it does it. I don't know that that's good advice, but it is common advice," Sarah said.

Brother Thomas smiled.

"I don't think that it is good advice," Michael said.

"I have my own reasons for thinking that, but why do you say so?" Sarah asked.

"There are some good practical reasons why not. It limits what you can do quite substantially. Knowledge lurks around every corner, and under every rock. I think that's at the heart of why C.S. Lewis said that if a man wishes to remain an atheist, he can't be too careful in selecting what he reads. But much more importantly, laboring under delusions tends to make one vulnerable to disillusionment. If you love an idea, rather than a real thing, your love becomes too easily contingent on how the thing makes you feel," Michael said.

"Four-fifths of the world thinks that's the only valid reason for loving something," Sarah said.

"So much the worse for the world," Michael said.

Sarah laughed.

"I imagine that a university might offer especially strong contrasts between its image and the underlying reality. How long has it been since you got your degree?" she asked Sonia.

"About eight months," Sonia said.

"And you've been working in the president's office, which these days deals more with the outside world than the inside world," Sarah said.

"I have. I've heard the occasional complaint, but I think I saw more of the seamy underside of Yalevard when I was a grad student—I was a teaching assistant, and reported several undergrads for cheating," Sonia said.

"Ah, but that's different. There's always a mystique about teachers. It's probably biggest when you're a kid, but even so there's just a huge gulf between the teacher and the student. It can't be crossed even if either side wanted it to be. Which neither side does," Sarah said.

"And these days the image and reality have an especially large disconnect since the image comes from another time and place," Brother Thomas said.

"How do you mean?" Sonia asked.

"Universities were originally medieval institutions. They were set up by the teachers to whom students flocked for the sake of learning. In the beginning there were no degrees. I mean the real beginnings, which you can trace fairly directly, in concept if not necessarily in execution, to the Lyceum of Aristotle and the Academy of Plato and the students that hung about Socrates. Europe is colder than Greece, so they used buildings for shelter, but it was the same idea. The disinterested pursuit of truth merely for the love of truth," Brother Thomas said.

"Of course, even in the ancient world erudition might be a career," Michael said.

"True. But if it was a career, it was not an industry," Brother Thomas answered.

"It's only an industry among those who treat it that way," Sarah said.

"If you'll pardon me, that seems to be most people in it," Brother Thomas said.

"That may be, but the Church wouldn't cease to be a church even if most people are there merely so their neighbors won't gossip. In the same way, there are those of us here who are here because we love knowledge, and want to pass on what we've learned. Perhaps between us we make the shadow that so many hide in because the university offers a comfortable life. But a living thing can support many parasites, and it is not the duty of a host to die in order to kill the parasites," she said with a smile.

"Well put," Brother Thomas said.

"None of which makes it any easier," Sonia said.

Sarah smiled sympathetically.

"There was a famous bicyclist who, answering a question from a journalist about cycling, said, 'It doesn't get any easier, you just go faster.' It seems to me that that describes an awful lot of life: it doesn't get any easier, you just get better at it."

"In Sonia's defense, Dean Floden seems to have been a lot worse than even I expected. Rum in a mini fridge in his office, pot delivered to his office by a student, sexually harassing several people, and at least two mistresses. Not that he was married, but none the less it seems the most accurate term," Brother Thomas said.

Sarah laughed.

"I think you'd have had trouble finding someone to give Jack a good character reference, even though none of us knew about his extracurricular activities," she said. "That being said, I don't think that he was bad so much as in as over his head, and had trouble at coping."

"Not many men are bad in good circumstances," Michael said.

"True enough. I suppose that's why the Lord's prayer includes 'lead us not into temptation'," Sarah said.

"It's not just Dean Floden that's been such an eye-opener. One bad man might happen anywhere. But the way the provost dealt with the complaints of sexual harassment against him! Her concern in everything related to Jack, in life and in death, is the reputation of the university. And Tiffany... I never imagined how cynical she is. And there's a professor who seduced one of her grad students and got him to try to kill Jack, even though it's not what got him. This place is a mess," Sonia said.

"It is. Easy living can do that to you. When things go your way too much, you can get lax and let things get worse because it's easier than dealing with the problems," Sarah said.

"Do you think that's what did it?" Sonia asked.

"In part. Human evil is never explicable apart from the choices that people make, but it is legitimate to ask what conditions encourage bad decisions and let them go unchecked," Sarah said.

"It is one of the most curious questions to ask when things have gone bad. How the people who did the bad stuff have screwed up, is obvious enough. But what of the good people who gave the bad ones the power they abused?" Michael said.

It was not a rhetorical question, but no one answered it.

"President Blendermore's theory is that money is the root of most evil in universities today," Brother Thomas said, in the silence that followed Michael's question.

"What people do in order to get grants, or relaxing standards to get tuition from more students?" Sarah asked.

"Not the chasing of money; the having of it. At first I thought he meant that money is power, and power corrupts. Interestingly, he didn't. His theory is that with money being so plentiful, all sorts of people are here who should not be: it's not just bank robbers who go where the money is," Brother Thomas said.

"Where the corpse is: there you will find the vultures," Brother Francis said.

"Now that's an interesting take on the problem," Sarah said.

"There's much to be said for that view," said Michael. "When the pope said to Saint Dominic, 'No longer can Peter say, "Gold and silver have I none",' Dominic hit the nail on the head when he replied, 'No, and neither can he say rise and walk.'"

Brother Thomas laughed and Brother Francis chuckled.

"I don't entirely get the reference, but that sounds somewhat disrespectful," Sonia said, surprised.

"It isn't at all," Brother Thomas said.

"The Church was founded by one perfect man, and contained one perfect woman, his mother. *Everyone* in the Church is painfully aware that that is an exhaustive list," Michael said.

"It's the sort of joke one makes about family. It doesn't mean that you love them less. It actually means that you love them more. It's because it's safe that you can be so honest," Sarah said.

"Are you Catholic?" Sonia asked Sarah.

"Didn't you notice the crucifix above the archway as you came in from the vestibule, the rosary on the kitchen counter, and the portrait of Saint Therese of Lisieux on the wall?" Brother Thomas asked.

"I didn't, but anyway I don't like to assume," Sonia said.

"Yes, I'm Catholic, as is Peter, though he's Byzantine-rite Catholic," Sarah said.

"If you paid attention to the conversation, she also upheld the validity of reason and the ability of the mind to reach truth, which these days are almost exclusively Catholic concepts," Michael said.

"The Eastern Orthodox hold them too," Sarah said.

"Hence the 'almost,'" Michael said.

"In fairness, you will find some Protestant sects upholding the validity of reason too, and more upholding it when they're not busy denying it," Brother Thomas said.

Michael shrugged his shoulders.

"Not to open a hornet's nest without gloves, but isn't a university founded on the idea that reason works?" Sonia asked.

"Yes," Michael said.

"It depends on what you mean by 'founded'," Sarah said.

"I assume that you mean that in a non-hair-splitting sense?" Sonia asked.

"Definitely. Were universities historically founded by people who believed that you could reach truth through reason? Yes. Does a university make no sense apart from that belief? Absolutely. Does the modern university live according to that belief? Imperfectly," Sarah said.

"But math depends entirely on reason," Sonia said.

"Technically it depends on reason for its internal validity," Peter cut in, "But it makes no claims about being able to know anything about the real world. All of math is conditional. *If* you have the natural numbers and *if* you have division, *then* you must have infinitely many numbers evenly divisible only by one and themselves. But it makes no claims whatsoever as to *whether* you have any natural numbers. Suppose that you have a prime number of pigeons greater than two. Then if you had one more pigeon, you would not have a prime number of pigeons. But that's equally true whether or not you have any pigeons at all. It tells me something about you *if* I already know something about you, but it doesn't tell me anything about you which is not already contained in my knowledge of you. It gives me no way to learn *new* things about you."

"I see what you mean," Sonia said.

"That's why, when statisticians aren't around, I define statistics as the misapplication of probability to the real world," Peter added, smiling.

"What do you mean? Statistics seems pretty successful," Sonia asked.

"Well, if you look at the definitions of probability which statisticians use, the real world never satisfies any of them. Technically, the statisticians are successful until they're not, and then everyone forgets it afterwards. Like how one-hundred-year floods happen every twenty to thirty years," Peter said.

"All probability distributions are approximations, of course-" Sonia said.

"No, it's not just that," Peter interrupted. "Look at the definition of probability that's used: the probability of a coin coming up heads is point-five because if you flip a coin forever, the limit of the number of times it comes up heads divided by the number of times you flip it is one half."

"And for us non-mathematicians?" Sarah asked.

"Eventually the number gets closer and closer to one half," Sonia said.

"Let's give the proper technical definition, because it illustrates my point," Peter said. "If you write down the results of every coin flip as you flip it infinitely many times, for any distance away from zero-point-five, there exists a place in the series where ever after, the number of heads divided by the number of coin flips never goes further away from zero-point-five than that distance. Now, I say this complicated definition not because I think it will make sense, but because it shows just how *unrelated* to real life the definition is. First, no one flips a coin infinitely many times. Second, no one cares that eventually, possibly long after the sun grows cold, the proportions of heads will be less than some small number away from zero-point-five. Or that some time probably much later, it will eventually stay even closer. Third, no one has ever proved that coins actually behave this way. We define a "Fair coin" to be one where the limit of heads divided by the total is equal to the limit of tails divided by the total is equal to zero-point-five. Reach into your pocket and pull out a coin. Is it a fair coin? Who knows? There's no way of finding out in a finite amount of time.

"So we just assume that coins are fair, and answers to surveys are normally distributed and it works as long as it works. Then when it doesn't, we call it bad luck or an act of God or just do our best to forget that it ever happened."

Having realized how long he'd been talking, Peter shrugged deprecatingly.

"I'm sorry, I'm not trying to give a classroom lecture, this is just sort of a pet peeve of mine," he said.

"I'm rather curious, now, of your opinion on Descartes' attempt to prove the validity of sense experience," Michael said.

"I must confess that I never read it. I tend to leave the philosophy to Sarah, and she just tells me the important bits," Peter said.

"One of the big questions philosophers were wrestling with during the 1600s was whether sense experience can be trusted," Sarah said. "Though they didn't put it in these terms, they were essentially asking if we could know for sure whether we were just brains in jars with electrodes faking all of our sensory input. Descartes attempted to prove, mathematically, that we could know that we weren't just brains in jars."

"That's why he started with *cogito ergo sum*—I think, therefore I am. He wanted to begin with some premise that could not possibly be doubted," Michael added.

"He chose well," Peter said.

"Not that some people haven't doubted it anyway," Brother Thomas said.

"Really?" Peter asked.

"The basic insight that the Buddha had was that he didn't really exist, and thus could escape the cycle of reincarnation," Brother Thomas said.

"So you're saying that Buddhists don't believe that they exist?" Peter asked.

"Oh no. Original Buddhism did not last very long. It changed quite substantially when it left India, and as I understand it Buddhism is all but dead in India," Brother Thomas said.

"Huh," Peter said.

"There are some curious similarities between Buddhism

and Modern Philosophy—the school of thought which Descartes accidentally started," Michael said.

"Do you really think that it was an accident?" Sarah asked.

* * *

The conversation continued like this through dinner, and after dinner into the small hours of the night. They were so caught up in the pleasure of each other's company that they forgot when the New Year's ball was going to drop and left the television off. The one exception was Brother Thomas, who always kept at least one eye out for details and had a keen sense of what time it was. He just didn't care about the ball dropping.

It was he who finally, at around one thirty, called attention to the time, as he had been texting Ian to make sure that they were not staying out past when Ian and his family were going to bed. While he was often quite absent-minded when it came to practical matters such as laundry, cleaning his room, and doing his taxes, he was scrupulous as a guest in somebody's home.

They took their leave reluctantly, after extensive thanks for the hospitality that they received, and set off towards home.

"May we walk you home?" Michael asked Sonia.

"Despite all the things we've learned, this campus is actually pretty safe," Sonia said.

"I'm sure it is. I was thinking more about the fact that at night when it's below freezing, it's as well to have someone make sure that your door lock hasn't frozen solid. The cold does not discriminate amongst its victims, except by numbers. We three will be going on together, while you would be alone," Michael said.

"For someone so philosophical, you can be very practical," Sonia said.

Michael shrugged his shoulders. "Hunting is intensely practical. I study philosophy, and I hunt. You study math and wear fashionable clothes. The one doesn't seem to be any more a contradiction than the other," he said.

Sonia laughed.

"There are plenty of people who wouldn't understand either of us," she said.

"That's possible," he admitted, then paused. "But I try to avoid estimating what other people understand."

Sonia wasn't entirely satisfied with that answer. It occurred to her that what she said could have been taken as flirting, which she didn't mean. It was late, and between the number of hours past her normal bedtime and the exhilaration of having a good time with new friends she was feeling slightly drunk. Though in fact no one had remembered to bring out champagne and the wine she had with dinner had long since left her blood. She decided to be more cautious in her reply.

"That sounds like a good policy. Well, since it is quite cold, and I'm tired enough that I might fall asleep on the way home, I think I'll accept your offer. You always get home faster if you don't do it by way of the hospital, as my mother would say," she said.

Accordingly, they all walked to Sonia's apartment. Her key did give a bit of trouble in the lock, requiring her to jiggle it slightly to get the lock to open, but gave way after a little trying. She bid them, and they bid her, a good night, and she went in. After closing the door, she went straight to her bed, laid down on it, and fell asleep in her coat and boots.

The brothers and Michael walked to President Blendermore's house where Ian—in pajamas, but obviously not
tired—let them in. He asked after their progress, and Brother
Thomas described the results of the day, including their eval-
uation of Dr. Marten and Paresh's failed attempt to kill the
dean. He listened without interrupting, and merely thanked
Brother Thomas at the end of the recital.

As they were getting ready for bed, Ian was very apol-
ogetic that he didn't have another guest bed for Michael.
Michael declined the offer of the couch, however, pleading
that between the thickness of the carpet, his ability to sleep
anywhere, and the fact that his height made sleeping on most
couches a cramped affair, he would be quite content on the
floor. After Ian tried a few other suggestions, Michael ended
up sleeping on the floor in Brother Thomas's room under a
spare blanket.

Chapter 8

Brother Thomas was the first to wake in the morning, at seven o'clock, and spent some time taking stock of the things they had learned. How to proceed was a good question, given that it was New Year's Day. Most businesses would be closed and most people in even less of a mood to talk to detectives than normal.

He revolved in his mind all of the clues which they had found and the possible motives they had discovered. He also considered the odd problem of the two people who were prevented from murder in equal parts by the real murderer and their own incompetence.

"Have you decided to trace the syringes yet?" Michael asked. Brother Thomas had not noticed him wake up, but Michael hadn't yet moved beyond opening his eyes.

"More or less. How long have you been awake?" Brother Thomas asked.

"Only a few moments, but clearly you'd been awake longer, and any fool would know what would be on your mind," Michael said.

"So the syringes are the key?" Thomas asked.

"Clearly. They're not necessary for figuring out who did it, based on what you've told me so far, but they're very necessary to proving it. And unlike your usual cases, being able to prove it is the most important thing," Michael said.

"I suppose it is," Brother Thomas said.

"It's bothering you that so much of this case is hinging on accidental evidence, isn't it?" Michael asked.

"It is," Brother Thomas admitted.

He was silent for a few moments, then added, "The physical evidence is very scant, and what we have we have by luck."

"What did you expect? If the murderer left evidence, he had to have done it by mistake. The murderer's mistakes are our good luck. Did you think it's possible to catch a murderer who does everything perfectly?" Michael asked.

"In theory it should be," Brother Thomas said.

"I don't think so. For one thing, the presence of evidence of any kind is, definitionally, a mistake on the murderer's part. I suppose you could have a perfect crime which is solvable by the motive. But as you know very well, the presence of motive is not enough to build a case for the very simple reason that plenty of people don't give into temptation. Otherwise every man with an ugly wife and a pretty friend would be automatically guilty of adultery. But you know better than I do that almost all of them are faithful."

Brother Thomas didn't respond, but he looked disappointed.

"You investigate a crime on the theory that everyone makes mistakes. Otherwise, there'd be nothing to investigate," Michael said.

"You're right, of course," Brother Thomas said.

"It's true that being lucky means that solving the case isn't proof of how smart you are," Michael said, gently.

Brother Thomas sighed.

"You know me too well," he said.

"You know me pretty well too," Michael said.

"Do you want me to save you the trouble of quoting *A Man for All Seasons*? 'If I were a teacher who would know?' 'You. Your students. Your friends. God. Not a bad audience, lad'," Brother Thomas said.

Michael smiled.

"You do the work because the work is worth doing. There's no shame in hoping for something extra. I know disappointment won't stop you from doing the work, and for the right reasons."

"Thanks," Brother Thomas said.

"Shall we go get breakfast? I'm hungry," Michael said.

"Such impudence must support a mighty appetite," Brother Thomas quoted, from a different movie.

⁂ ⁂ ⁂

Michael, who was a good judge of character, correctly guessed that Ian would not mind if he made free with the kitchen so long as he cleaned up afterwards and didn't scratch the non-stick pans. To sweeten the deal, he made eggs, bacon, and rich, buttery pancakes for everyone in the house. He even had the principle pans and bowls cleaned up by the time Ian and Staci came down. Even a grouchy host cannot complain when he wakes up to the smell of bacon and pancakes, and the Blendermores were, by both inclination and principle, gracious hosts. Brother Francis came to breakfast right behind them.

The conversation over breakfast might have turned to the

case at hand, had Michael not discovered that Ian's first PhD was in philosophy. Though Michael had strong principles, he had a still stronger hunger for good conversation. In this case it got the better of him. Ian, it turned out, had a special interest in early Roman philosophers, whom Michael had not spent much time studying. He questioned Ian rather minutely about them through breakfast.

When breakfast was nearly over, there was a knock on the door. Staci answered it, and opened the door to Sonia.

"Hi, do you mind if I come in? Are the brothers here?" she asked.

"Please do, and yes, they're here. And Happy New Year! Have you eaten anything? You're in time for breakfast," Staci replied, ushering her in out of the cold.

"I haven't," Sonia admitted as she came in and smelled the food.

"Well come grab a plate. There's still plenty left. Michael made it, actually, and he seems to think that we all have the appetite of lumberjacks," Staci joked.

Sonia bid everyone a good morning and happy new year as she came into the dining room.

"I didn't mean to interrupt, but I texted Brother Thomas to ask what the plans were for the day and he didn't reply, so I figured I should stop over here to catch you guys before you go off without me," Sonia said.

She thought this needed further explanation, especially so soon after the night before, so she added, "I've come this far with you in the investigation, I don't want to miss out now."

"Having fun?" Staci asked.

"Fun isn't the right word, but it is very interesting," Sonia said.

"It is a bit of excitement," Staci said. "Universities have a lot in common with the giant oaks that grow on their lawns. There's a lot going on, though you don't really see it from the ground. Every now and then the wind blows through and the thing moves a little, but not very much, and the wind lets up, and the tree goes back to doing what it was doing as if nothing happened. Don't get me wrong. Sometimes the wind breaks off a branch, but if you're not sitting on the branch you're not really going to notice. The investigation is like being in the tree when the wind blows."

Brother Thomas noticed Ian looking at Staci with admiration, and approved. It was nice to see people in another vocation showing the good side of it.

"That's an interesting analogy. I'm used to hearing universities described as giant machines," Brother Francis said.

"I'm a biologist. I don't know much about machines. And machines are built with a purpose. Universities, like trees, grow up in response to their environment and what the other parts of them are doing. A fungal colony or a coral reef would probably be a more direct analogy, but I like trees better," Staci said.

There was a brief silence as people considered what she said but had nothing to add.

"So what are we up to today? I assume that we're not going to take the day off just because it's New Year's?" Sonia asked. She had the mathematician's disdain for celebrating the cycling of numbers according to arbitrarily chosen bases.

"Of course not," Brother Thomas said.

"Though we may find that everyone else is taking the day off," Brother Francis said.

"That is a risk we run, but I fancy that at least one witness will be available," Brother Thomas said.

"Who?" Brother Francis asked.

145

"Did any of you notice the logo on the syringes?" Brother Thomas asked.

"It was the name of some business, wasn't it?" Brother Francis asked.

"I don't think that I even see logos anymore. They're on everything," Sonia said.

"It's the name of a veterinary practice," Brother Thomas said.

"Local?" Brother Francis asked.

"Just twenty-five minutes away in Macedonia," Brother Thomas said.

Macedonia was the nearest city to Yalevard. It was in fact the site of where the first classes of Yalevard were taught before Cornelius Yalevard endowed the nascent university with a campus in 1847.

"What makes you think they'll be open?" Brother Francis asked.

"I looked them up, and they have an emergency clinic as part of their practice. There are three veterinarians who work there, two of them being co-owners. In my experience, emergency clinics are always staffed on holidays, especially when they serve a large area. The next closest veterinarian is forty miles away," Brother Thomas said.

"Do you think that the emergency staff is likely to know anything?" Sonia asked.

"The great thing about small practices is that the emergency staff and the regular staff are the same people. Though, of course, you never know exactly who you're going to get. We can but try," Brother Thomas said.

"Couldn't we call to find out who's there?" Sonia asked.

"It's much harder to turn people away who have showed up at your doorstep. Unless, that is, they've been foolish enough to call ahead so that you can say, 'I'm sorry you wasted your time, but like I said on the phone, I'm busy and I don't know anything,'" Brother Thomas said.

"I forgot how much you manipulate people as a detective," Sonia said.

"If people were all saints, the life of a detective would be at once much easier and completely unnecessary. But manipulation is only bad when you're manipulating someone into doing the wrong thing. When it benefits the person, it's properly called 'being helpful'," Brother Thomas said.

"And does your manipulation benefit these people?" Sonia asked.

"If you worked at a veterinarian's office, would your life be better for having helped to catch a murderer, or for having gotten your work done a few minutes earlier?" Brother Thomas asked.

"I see your point, though it does seem self-serving," Sonia said.

"If I believed I was doing wrong, I would go into a different line of work. When the truth is inconvenient, you should do something else," Brother Thomas said.

"Ready answers always sound suspicious, but Brother Thomas has been doing this for years. If you get asked questions often enough, you can't help but refine the answer with each time you give it," Michael said.

Sonia smiled.

"I wasn't trying to accuse you of anything. I just haven't gotten used to this yet," she said to Brother Thomas.

"With luck, you won't have to," he said.

* * *

It had snowed overnight again. Sonia offered to drive, as she had a four-wheel drive vehicle with studded tires on it. They fit into the car surprisingly well, given that Michael was six foot four and Brother Thomas six foot one. Brother Thomas was, however, very thin, and Michael very flexible, and so they could both take up surprisingly little space.

The trip was an easy one, which anyone who lived around Yalevard was used to making. The studded tires meant that it took place with a medium-pitched rumble the entire way, but that was far less unpleasant than periodically skidding, especially in cross-winds over bridges.

The clinic was easy to find, and had five cars parked in its lot, only one of which turned out to have brought a patient. The veterinarian on call was a Dr. Metcalf, one of the owners, and was busy with a cat who had been brought in after eating a Christmas ornament made of loose yarn. However, a vet tech was available.

"Can I help you?" she asked, after the receptionist paged her to the front desk. She was in her late twenties, with light brown hair tied in a functional ponytail and a long sleeve t-shirt on under her medical scrubs despite the heater being turned up.

"Hello," Brother Thomas said.

He had trouble reading her, for some reason, and so he went with the most direct approach. It is always easier to apologize for excessive honesty than for flexibility with the truth.

"My name is Brother Thomas, and this is Brother Francis."

He produced a card, which he handed to her.

"These are our associates, Dr. Sonia Olivera and Mr. Michael Chesterton."

The vet tech, whose name tag bore the name Rachel, read the card but didn't register much of a reaction. She looked up and waited for some request to be made.

"You may have heard that there was a death at Yalevard a few days ago? Specifically Jack Floden, Dean of the College of Liberal Arts and Sciences?"

"Yeah, Jenny told me about that when she read it in the newspaper," Rachel said.

"Some syringes were found at the scene which had your logo on them," Brother Thomas said.

He showed her one of the pictures he had taken in which the clinic's logo was clear.

"That's one of the new ones we got in," Rachel said.

"New ones?"

"We recently switched suppliers, and the new needles look pretty different from the old ones. We've only been using those about two weeks," she said.

"Really? How interesting. Tell me, what do you give them out for?" Brother Thomas asked.

"Mostly just diabetes in cats and dogs. There are other conditions which might call for it, but we don't have any patients with those right now. Did someone kill this Floden guy by injecting him with insulin we gave him for his dog?" Rachel asked.

"Do you mean that Dean Floden had a diabetic dog you treated?" Brother Thomas asked.

"No, I don't think he had any pets that were patients here. Jenny would know, and I think she would have said when she told me," Rachel said.

"Do you treat many diabetic pets?" Brother Thomas asked.

"Not too many. We don't see it too often around here,

and outside the university a lot of people will put a dog or cat down if they learn that it's going to cost hundreds of dollars a year in vet bills. It's sad, but a lot of people around here don't have a lot of money. I mean, what are you gonna do?" she said.

"Would it be possible to get a list of the people who might have gotten these needles? As you might imagine, it's critical to track down where the murder weapons came from," Brother Thomas said.

"Are you working for the police?" Rachel asked.

"No, we're working for the university. You might say that we're working with the police, and certainly anything you give us we'll give them a copy of. It would, however, be incorrect to assume that we act with their authority," Brother Thomas said.

"I don't know. There might be some confidentiality issue. I mean, I don't know whether there is such thing as veterinary confidentiality—it's never come up before. It's not like it's anybody else's business whose pets are sick, but I don't know whether there's any laws about it, either. I really can't make that call. You'll have to ask Doctor Metcalf," Rachel said.

As luck would have it, Dr. Metcalf came out to give the person with the cat the news that the surgery had been completed successfully, and that the cat was resting.

Once this was over and the person was handed over to the receptionist for payment, Rachel caught Dr. Metcalf's attention and called him over. He was a thin, athletic-looking man, clean shaven, with short wavy brown hair. Perhaps forty-five, he looked like he was into some sort of outdoorsy sport like running or cycling.

She summarized the request, and Brother Thomas added

some clarifying information to help swing the decision in the right direction.

"There are no laws which govern confidentiality like there are with human medicine, and we don't really make any promises to our patients' owners," Dr. Metcalf said. "I mean, it wouldn't be good for us if people thought that we were talking behind their backs or giving out their information... I mean, everyone expects a certain amount of privacy. But this is a pretty unusual circumstance... I think that most people wouldn't mind... You know what, let me ask Jenny to make the list and I'll look at it and see what I think."

Brother Thomas thanked him, and he walked over to the receptionist, who had finished with the cat owner. He spoke with her for perhaps two minutes, then wrote a few things down on a sticky note and came back, holding it.

"It turns out that there were only a few people who got syringes from us that would have been from the new batch, between going through previous stock and canceled appointments because it's been snowing so much lately," Dr. Metcalf said.

"That's convenient," Brother Thomas said.

"If you'll agree that you're interested in someone who lives near the university, I can eliminate the client who lives forty-five minutes in the other direction?" Dr. Metcalf asked.

"That seems like a reasonable assumption, at least at this stage," Brother Thomas said.

"In that case there are two people who we gave them to that you would be interested in," he said, and handed Brother Thomas the sticky note.

"Thank you. Just to be thorough, is there any chance that syringes might have been stolen from here?" Brother Thomas asked.

"I can't conclusively rule it out. Syringes by themselves aren't a controlled substance. You can buy them on the internet without a prescription. So we don't keep them under lock and key with careful inventorying. I mean, they're worth less than a dollar each, so it's not like they'd ordinarily be a high theft item. We *do* keep targets for theft in the building, though, so it's got good locks and a security system. And before you ask, there haven't been any break-ins in the last year," Dr. Metcalf said.

"And customers would not normally get a chance to steal anything, would they?" Brother Thomas asked.

"It's very unlikely. We keep all of the medical supplies in the same protected place, and as I said since we do have some targets for theft, we're careful about it. You need keys which we keep in our pockets, not hanging up on the wall," Dr. Metcalf said.

"And just to be completely thorough, would the staff be able to take syringes without anyone knowing?" Brother Thomas asked.

"I'm sure that it wouldn't be hard for us to do, but none of us live near the university, or really have anything to do with it," he said.

"Thank you. I'm confident it isn't any of you, but as long as I'm taking up your time now, it's best to be thorough rather than having to come back. Thank you very much for your assistance. You might well have helped us to catch a murderer," Brother Thomas said.

"Good luck. And if I did, please make sure that their pet goes to a good home," Dr. Metcalf said.

"To the degree that it will be within my power, I will," Brother Thomas said.

"Goodbye," Dr. Metcalf said.

"God be with you," Brother Thomas said.

When they had gotten into the car, Sonia turned out to be the one whose curiosity could not wait.

"Well, what are the names on the list?" she asked.

"Li Xiaoping and... Frank Buskirk," Brother Thomas said.

"Who is Li Xiaoping?" Brother Francis asked.

"He's a professor in the College of Engineering," Brother Thomas said.

"Which makes it very unlikely that he had anything to do with Dean Floden," Sonia said.

"Indeed," Brother Thomas agreed.

"Does this mean that we've solved the case?" Sonia asked.

"I think we know who did it. We haven't solved the case in the sense of having a solution," Brother Thomas said.

"What do you mean? Isn't 'who did it' the solution?" Sonia asked.

"This is very circumstantial evidence. We need real proof that Buskirk did it," Brother Thomas said.

"What sort of proof can there be?" Sonia asked.

"That is an excellent question," Brother Thomas said.

They were silent for a moment, and Sonia started the car, pulled out of the parking space, and started driving back to the university.

"A witness would be ideal, of course, but aside from us not having a witness, I think a witness is essentially impossible because of the blizzard. Apart from everyone staying inside, I gather that the visibility was twenty or thirty feet. Buskirk could have ambushed Floden while wearing a clown suit and been safe," Brother Thomas said.

"Do we have any idea how Buskirk got Floden to go back to his office?" Sonia asked.

"An idea occurs to me," Brother Francis said. "If Buskirk

did it, this is clearly a case of revenge for Floden having sabotaged him in the matter of the research grant."

"Granted a grant is important, but people don't get grants all the time. Is that really worth killing over?" Sonia asked.

"If Buskirk's emails to Dean Floden are to be believed, it was the grant of a lifetime. Buskirk was amazed that he got it, and then it was—effectively—snatched out from under him. He'd won the lottery, and Dean Floden burned the ticket," Brother Thomas said.

"How?" Sonia asked.

"The university takes sixty percent of every grant. I forget what they call it. Administrative overhead, or something. I don't have a great memory for euphemisms. Anyway, the grant was conditional on the university taking only forty percent. Buskirk applied for an exception to be made in his case, but Floden fought it. It wasn't completely clear from the emails that I saw, but basically Floden lead Buskirk to believe that he was escalating the matter to the provost, when in fact he never mentioned it to her. He strung Buskirk along, then finally told him that no exception was going to be made. The deadline had just passed on Friday," Brother Thomas said.

"What a bastard!" Sonia said.

Brother Thomas let that pass without comment.

"Buskirk would have been getting revenge, but contrary to the movies, revenge is not a personal thing," Brother Francis said. "It is, of course, but it's not usually justified that way. Instead, the person seeking revenge says that their revenge is justice. Floden was an evil man, and there's no justice in the world, and Buskirk was finally going to bring justice to somebody. The world would be better off without Jack Floden. Jack Floden would never again ruin someone's life. That sort of thing. Buskirk would have been a man on a mission. So I think that night, in the blizzard and everything, he was stalking his prey. He hid somewhere outside of Floden's house, but not far, staring in as if to see through the walls and figure out how to rid the world of the monster inside. And what would he have seen Friday night?"

"Audrey!" Brother Thomas said.

"Exactly. The night was ripe for killing, but Floden would never open his door to Buskirk. Here was an opportunity to make Floden go wherever Buskirk wanted," Francis said.

"He blackmailed him. Anonymously, do you think?," Brother Thomas said.

"Probably, but it doesn't matter. If he wanted Floden to reverse his decision, Floden would have had to go along to talk to him just as much as if he wanted money. Still, I think he pretended to want money," Brother Francis said.

"Hi Jack. I just saw your playmate leave. It wouldn't be good for your career if you banging a student got out. I'll meet you at your office in an hour. We can talk about what it will cost to keep my mouth shut. Leave the front door open and don't turn on the lights. Click," Brother Francis said in a raspy, breathy voice that would have been hard to identify. It was a chilling demonstration.

"I think you're right. But if that's what happened, I don't see how we can get any evidence of it," Brother Thomas said.

"The police might get call logs from the nearby payphones to see whether they called Floden's house. I can't imagine that they're used very often," Brother Francis said.

"When we next speak with the sheriff, we'll mention the suggestion. But that's not evidence which we can collect, and in any event a phone call to Floden's house from a payphone would not prove that Buskirk was the one who made it," Brother Thomas said.

"True. It is nice to get confirmation of whatever you can, though," Brother Francis said.

"It is. But let's proceed on the assumption that you're correct. What would happen next? Presumably he didn't already have the plan fully formed and waiting for an event he couldn't have expected," Brother Thomas said.

"No, I think the plan came to him when he saw Audrey leave Floden's house," Brother Francis said.

"But why Floden's office? Why not a lonely field or someplace in the woods?" Sonia asked.

"Have you ever been in a lonely field? They feel amazingly public when you're in them, no matter how alone you are," Brother Thomas said.

"How about a secluded place in the woods. I mean, there's no chance that you'd run into someone who was out for a hike in a blizzard," Sonia said.

"First, you never know. Any place where strangers might go feels more public than it is when you're contemplating doing something there you really don't want to be caught doing. Second, giving directions in the woods is harder than you think, especially in the dark. You can't murder someone who doesn't show up because he couldn't find the forked tree with the broken branch and decided to go home and have some hot cocoa instead," Brother Thomas said.

"You'd be amazed what doesn't seem so bad after all, when you're in the woods and it's dark and cold," Michael added.

"Also, it would just be unpleasant. Murderers like comfort as much as anyone else," Brother Thomas added.

"I think that there may have been a symbolic value to the office," Brother Francis said.

"Killed where he did his evil, that the walls that witnessed so much injustice might finally witness justice?" Brother

Thomas asked.

"Something like that. It occurs to me that those missing pictures might be something personal and important to Floden, which were connected to him as a dean," Brother Francis said.

"Do you think Dean Floden was the sort of man to display his diplomas on the wall? There were none in that office," Brother Thomas said.

"I think he was. Diplomas are exactly the sort of thing that an avenging warrior would have taken," Brother Francis said.

"Let us hope, then, that if Buskirk did take them, he has not yet destroyed them. He's certainly had the time," Brother Thomas said.

"Why would he keep them?" Sonia asked.

"Distressingly few answers present themselves," Brother Francis said.

"To return to the previous question, what did Buskirk do right after he saw Audrey come out of Floden's house?" Brother Thomas asked.

"I think he went straight to the phone. He saw the opportunity and jumped on it. Always open Christmas presents immediately, especially late ones," Brother Francis said.

"And then?" Thomas asked.

Brother Francis shut his eyes, putting himself on that snowy street in his imagination.

"I think he went home to carefully think through his plan, in the warmth, where he'd be less likely to overlook something," Brother Francis said.

"And so we come to the big question: where did he get the heroin?" Brother Thomas asked.

"Couldn't he have just bought it for the purpose?" Sonia

suggested.

"How would he have known where to get it?" Brother Thomas asked.

"Maybe he used the stuff himself," Sonia said.

"I don't think that he's a heroin addict. He doesn't have any of the signs," Brother Thomas said.

"Does that really eliminate the possibility of him having procured the heroin himself?" Brother Francis asked.

"No," Brother Thomas said, "There are indirect ways of knowing things as well as direct ways. He might know Jordan or some other heroin dealer socially. He might have met the heroin dealer when he was helping a client, if he practices. There are all sorts of ways he could have accidentally learned where to get heroin. Coincidences do happen. And from his perspective it wouldn't even be a coincidence. If he didn't know where to get heroin—however he got it—he would have used something else, or not killed Floden at all. That's part of what makes a detective's life so difficult. You can't rationally deduce the strange coincidences that make up life, you can only deduce the things that logically follow each other, and hope that's enough."

"You can be very negative, sometimes," Sonia teased.

"I think that Chesterton—G.K., not Michael—would say that since we are finite creatures, to be negative is only to outline where we positively exist. Wouldn't he, Michael?" Brother Thomas asked.

"To be negative is to draw our outline? I don't know. Perhaps he would have. If he did, though, I think that he would have added that we should spend the main part of our effort coloring inside the lines," Michael said.

Brother Thomas laughed.

"Who is G.K. Chesterton?" Sonia asked.

"An English journalist in the early 1900s who said something about everything, and pretty much all of it worth listening to," Michael said.

"Are you any relation to him?" Sonia asked.

"Not that I know of, I regret to say. Given that we share the same surname, it is always possible that he and I are seventeenth cousins eight times removed, or something like that, but I know of no closer bond of blood than being members of the same species," Michael said.

"To get back to the question at hand," said Brother Thomas, "There are at least several other ways that Buskirk could have gotten the heroin. He could have bought some to try but never used it, he could have a roommate who uses heroin, he could have taken it off of someone either like how you take the keys from a drunk or as an opportunistic theft. He might have confiscated it from a student. It's even possible that some idiot handed it in to him with an assignment. Professors get all sorts of odd things turned in to them by accident."

"That's true," Sonia interjected. "When I was a teaching assistant I got two love notes—to other people—several assignments for other classes, and once a student even turned in her cheat sheet with her test. If assignments weren't purely paper, like in math, I could only imagine what might show up."

"It's also possible that Buskirk had been planning to kill Floden before he saw Audrey, and found some opportunity for stealing heroin without yet knowing how he was going to use it. If you're planning a murder, stealing the murder weapon from someone you don't know is a great way to distance yourself from it," Brother Thomas said.

"I can't say why, and it could be otherwise, but I don't

think that Buskirk was planning this for a long time," Brother Francis said.

"You're probably right. All the more reason I don't incline towards the idea that Buskirk bought the heroin that night after seeing Audrey," Brother Thomas said.

"Wouldn't that argue in the other direction?" Sonia asked.

"Buskirk doesn't seem like a complete idiot. Buying a deadly weapon hours before you're going to use it is both highly suggestive and very traceable. If I were going to murder someone, I would prefer to use an item I bought out of town, for cash, years ago. Stealing it in the dead of night with no witnesses, more than a decade ago, would be preferable, of course," Brother Thomas said.

"I see your reasoning," Brother Francis said.

"Unfortunately, the untraceable methods of having procured the heroin are... untraceable. We must therefore hope that he used one of the traceable methods," Brother Thomas said.

"So we're supposed to track down whether he purchased the heroin even though we think he didn't?" Sonia asked.

"Yes," Brother Thomas said.

"Isn't that a waste of time?" Sonia asked.

"I could easily be wrong about Floden having had it before that night. Sometimes people do stupid things. Sometimes people do strange things. Sometimes people do completely inexplicable things. 'There are more things in heaven and earth, Horatio, than are dreamt of in your philosophy'," Brother Thomas said.

"Hamlet was talking about ghosts," Brother Francis said.

"Yes, but ordinary people can be stranger than ghosts," Brother Thomas said.

"So does that make our next stop Jordan's house?" Sonia

asked.

"Actually, our next stop is the church. If we do anything else, we'd miss daily mass. Will you come with us again?" Brother Thomas asked.

"Sure, why not," Sonia said. She still hadn't figured out why she was going to mass with them, but by this point it was verging on being a habit.

They pulled into the church's parking lot not long after this exchange.

* * *

When mass was over, they got back into the car.

"Shall we drive over to Jordan's house, or should I park on campus and we'll walk?" Sonia asked.

"Actually, would you be able to drop me off at my car?" Michael asked.

"Is there somewhere you need to go?" Sonia asked.

"Home. I've done what I came up here to do, and while I've enjoyed the time I've spent here, I should get back to my students. There's no problem with leaving them in the care of my senior students for a short time, but that is a relationship which should not be abused," he said.

"You're not going to stay to see the case through?" Sonia asked, surprised.

Michael smiled.

"There's no need," he said.

"As you wish," Sonia said.

Accordingly, she drove to the parking lot where Michael's car was. It had several inches of snow on it, which the brothers and Sonia helped Michael to remove. When this was complete Michael started the car and let it run to warm up as he said goodbye.

He hugged Brother Thomas, shook hands with Brother Francis and offered Sonia his hand. She hesitated for a second, then shook it.

"It was a great pleasure meeting you," he said pleasantly.

"It was a great pleasure meeting you too. I guess you're not likely to come back up this way again?" Sonia asked.

"I can't say it seems likely to me. Hopefully you guys pick your next dean better than this one and he doesn't torture any psychologically vulnerable psychologists," Michael said.

"I'd like to think that the next one has to be better, but that's probably naive," Sonia said.

Michael smiled.

"If you ever want to come down and visit us, my sister would be happy to put you up in the guest bedroom at her place. Brother Thomas often forgets to make invitations, but he's always happy to have people come ask him what cases he's working on," he said.

"He's not wrong on either count," Brother Thomas said.

Sonia smiled.

"I think I will," she said.

"Until then," Michael said, and got in his car. He drove off with neither haste nor delay.

Sonia turned to Brother Thomas.

"To Jordan's?"

"Yes, but I think you're right that we should walk. It just seems more fitting in a university," Brother Thomas said.

* * *

They knocked on the door of the house with two Jordans, and at first got no answer. After a minute, they heard some movement inside. A minute later, the female Jordan answered the door again.

"Hello," she said, without committing herself to anything.

"Can we talk to you privately?" Sonia asked.

Jordan looked them over.

"I guess we can talk if you like, but I doubt I have any more intuitions I can share with you," she said.

"Thank you," Sonia said.

They walked in, and after closing the door Jordan led them to the couch on which she and Sonia had talked.

Brother Thomas took the lead this time.

"There is a question we didn't know to ask, the last time we spoke. It is not likely to be a question you will want to answer. So let me say in advance that if you give us the truth, we will do our best to keep the police from asking you the same question. And our best is likely to be good enough," he said.

Jordan thought this over.

"You can ask me anything you want. Whether I have an answer for you, and whether I'll give it to you if I do, depends on what you ask me," she said.

Brother Thomas saw what Sonia saw in Jordan. She was using her intelligence for bad purposes but she was a very clever young woman. He decided that being as oblique as possible would give her the maximum leeway to answer.

"Have you ever met a man by the name of Buskirk?" he asked.

Jordan's expression didn't waver.

"The name sounds familiar. I may have met him," she said.

It was becoming very clear that whatever information

they might get out of Jordan would be very deniable. Perhaps she believed that they wore secret recording devices. More likely, she was merely operating on the theory that if you never drop your guard you'll never be caught off guard.

"You know, it's not common knowledge, so please don't repeat this, but Dean Floden died of a massive heroin overdose. This means that the killer had to get heroin from somewhere," Brother Thomas said.

Jordan evidently found this interesting, but didn't see a question in it.

"We're wondering if the killer might have gotten the heroin from Buskirk," Brother Thomas said, venturing a little further into being explicit.

Jordan considered that for the better part of a minute.

"If Derek is the person I'm thinking of, I met him at a party. I believe he offered me some heroin. I refused, of course, but it wouldn't shock me if the killer got his heroin from Derek," Jordan said.

Brother Thomas admired the wordcraft, but his admiration didn't make him miss the name she used.

"Wait. Derek?" he asked.

"Derek Buskirk." Jordan said, perplexed, with the sort of clarity of pronunciation one uses when someone might have misheard.

"We were asking about Frank Buskirk," Brother Thomas said.

"Frank? I don't think I've ever heard of him," Jordan said.

"He's a professor at Yalevard. A psychology professor," Brother Thomas said.

"The Buskirk that I know is a landscaper, and too young to be a professor," Jordan said.

Brother Thomas had pulled up a photo on his phone of

Dr. Buskirk from his university faculty page and showed it to Jordan.

"No, that's definitely not the guy I know," she said.

"It seems unlikely that there would be more than one guy with the name Buskirk in town. I suppose we don't know that he didn't come from here, but his undergraduate degree was taken in California. Could the guy you know have given you a fake name?" Brother Thomas asked.

Jordan shrugged her shoulders.

"Guys can say anything they want at parties, and it's not like you're going to check up on them. On the other hand, I don't know of any guys I've met who've given me a fake name," she said.

"I don't suppose the guy... invited you back to his house, that you would know where he lives?" Brother Thomas asked.

Jordan paused to consider again.

"As a matter of fact, he did. I didn't go home with him, of course. But he did mention living above the Y-Mart," she said.

Brother Thomas looked at Sonia to see whether this was a place she recognized.

"It's a small convenience store on Main Street," she said.

Brother Thomas nodded.

"Thank you for your help," he said to Jordan, and stood up. Sonia and Brother Francis stood up as well. Jordan remained sitting.

"You're surprisingly realistic about life, for a monk," she said.

Brother Thomas smiled.

"You know, I really thought—when I saw you at the door, and you were the one talking instead of the beautiful lady— that you were going to appeal to my ideals. Ask me to do the right thing," she said.

"Do you have any ideals?" Brother Thomas asked. It was a genuine question, though asked dispassionately.

"I'd like to say that I do, but I can't think of any right now," Jordan said. It was equally dispassionate, neither bragging nor self-reproachful.

Brother Thomas shrugged.

"Ideals are dangerous in your line of work. The only thing I can think of that's more dangerous is not having any," he said.

Jordan laughed, softly.

"But that's only in the long run," he added.

"You might be right. But the long run is far away, and there's a lot of right now to get through before we get there."

"As someone more than ten years older than you, I'm supposed to tell you that it goes by in the blink of an eye. But it doesn't. There's a lot of time between now and then. Which is actually why what matters isn't savoring the time, it's using it well," Brother Thomas said.

"Do something you'll be proud of?" Jordan asked, a hint of mockery in her tone.

"Only in an accidental sense. If you do something in order to be proud of it, you'll have wasted your time," Brother Thomas said.

Jordan looked a little surprised.

"So what, then? Don't do anything you'll regret?" she asked, an echo of the former mocking appearing in her tone.

"I'm not big on avoiding emotional decisions in the present only by consulting one's emotions in the future," Brother Thomas said.

"Do your duty? Think of the people who depend on you, or who are going to depend on you? Lay a good foundation for the future?" Jordan guessed.

"None of those, though that last one is probably the least furthest away," Brother Thomas said.

"But I am laying a good foundation for the future, getting my degree without debt," Jordan said.

"In a financial sense, you're quite right. But I said it was the least far away, not that it was close," Brother Thomas said.

"Fine, I give up, then. What do you mean?" Jordan asked. She seemed genuinely interested. She did not often meet people she could not read. This may, of course, have been as much a reflection on the people she associated with as it was on Brother Thomas' readability.

"Our lives are made up of all the moments we have lived, and though we may forget the past, it is still a part of us. It is possible to acquire food allergies; it is also possible to acquire spiritual allergies. To draw an example at random, I have been told that raising children involves a great deal of dull work. There are years when you need to watch them to make sure they don't kill themselves, but they don't do or say anything very interesting. You can spend hours, grinding away at watching them grow up, and for the whole time you're not the most important person in the room. If you have grown spiritually allergic to dullness or unimportance, this may not be bearable."

"Would you have found it bearable?" Jordan asked.

"No," Brother Thomas said candidly, "But that's me. I suspect that Brother Francis would have been great at it."

He shifted to leave, then paused.

"I don't mean this as a warning. It's not even friendly advice. I just think that people should make the mistakes that they're going to make with their eyes open."

He stood up.

"It's been a pleasure talking with you, and I thank you for your help. God be with you," he said, bowing his head very slightly as he said the farewell, and walked to the door.

As he opened the door, Jordan called after him, "Thank you, Brother. It's... refreshing, to be taken seriously. If he exists, God be with you too."

Chapter 9

When they got outside and closed the door, Sonia was the first to speak. "How can you like someone and be afraid of them at the same time?"

"That gets to the heart of the difference between natural and moral virtue," Brother Thomas said.

"The difference between what and what?" Sonia asked.

"Natural and moral virtue. To be strong is a natural virtue. To use that strength to help people is a moral virtue. To use your strength to hurt people without provocation is a moral vice. To be weak could be called a natural vice, though that would be an uncommon usage. It would be more typical to say simply that you lack the natural virtue of strength," Brother Thomas said.

"Okay, I get the distinction. How does that apply to Jordan?" Sonia asked.

"She has an abundance of natural virtues. Intelligence and self control among them. Hence you like her. These virtues are in service of some things which seem suspiciously like moral vices. Hence the fear," Brother Thomas said. "Would you mind leading the way to the Y-Mart?,"

"I do believe that you're being impatient!" Sonia marvelled.

"I'm quite eager to see what we find there, but if you have any other philosophical questions, I or Brother Francis will happily answer them along the way," Brother Thomas said.

Sonia started walking.

"On a more concrete level, Jordan is scary because she seems to be honest with herself," Brother Francis said.

"She does seem to be unusually honest with herself, or at least about herself, but why should that make her scary?" Sonia asked.

"Because people who are honest with themselves act on principles, not instincts, and principles have sharp edges. In this case, if she's able to do what she does without lying to herself, there's no way to know where she'll draw the line. If there *is* anywhere she will draw the line. That's the problem with not knowing what her principles are," Brother Francis said.

They got to the Y-Mart in a few minutes, and took only a minute longer to discover the stairs to the apartment above it. The door locked at the bottom, as is sensible in any place with a high likelihood of having drunk people around. Brother Thomas pushed the doorbell button. Unfortunately, the button being so far from the apartment meant it was impossible to tell if it was working.

Brother Thomas stared at the door to the stairs as if concentrating hard enough might let him see whether anyone was inside. Just as he was about to consider whether the circumstances justified picking the lock, they heard the sound of footsteps descending the stairs. Which was just as well, since the answer would have been no.

The door opened and in it stood a youngish man in a grey

sweatshirt and blue sweatpants with curly brown hair and several days of untrimmed stubble. He looked at the people on the other side of it with irritated surprise.

"Yes?" he asked.

"Are you Derek Buskirk?" Brother Thomas asked.

"Yeah," he said.

"May we come in and speak with you privately?" Brother Thomas asked.

"I'm not interested in hearing about Jesus," Derek said, and started closing the door.

"That much is obvious," Brother Thomas said. He caught the door so it didn't close all the way and said, quietly, "We're here to talk to you about a white, powdery substitute for heaven which costs more and doesn't work as well, but which *is* available before you die."

Derek stopped pushing the door closed, but didn't open it.

"Are you selling or trying to buy?" he asked.

"I'd much rather be on the same side of a closed door as you before I say more," Brother Thomas said.

"I don't know you," Derek said.

"If you let me in for five minutes, it can stay that way. Keep me out, and you'll get to know me well when I'm visiting you in prison," Brother Thomas said.

"Are you a cop?" Derek asked.

"No. I'm a private detective, so I have the option of keeping my mouth shut if I want to. Staying on my good side would, therefore, be advisable," Brother Thomas said.

Derek muttered some random uncultured words to indicate his disapproval of the situation and let the door open. As he walked up the stairs to his apartment, he said over his shoulder, "Close the door on your way in."

They ascended the stairs and walked into the main room of Derek's apartment. It was about as slovenly as one would expect of a heroin addict in his mid-twenties who still manages to pay his rent. Sonia was glad it only looked bad, and didn't stink. Brother Thomas was pleased at how much of their information it confirmed.

"So what do you want?" Derek asked, with no attempt to hide his annoyance.

"Do you know Frank Buskirk?" Brother Thomas asked, his words measured but his tone sharp.

Derek scowled.

"I wish I didn't," he said.

Brother Thomas gestured for Derek to continue.

"He's my cousin."

"Why?" Brother Thomas asked.

"Because my father and his father are brothers," Derek said.

"Why do you wish you didn't know him?" Brother Thomas asked. His intensity was focused like a dagger at the young man who didn't want to talk with him.

"Because he stole from me," Derek said.

"What did he steal from you?" Brother Thomas asked.

Derek stared back at Brother Thomas.

"We know you do heroin, and we don't care. What did he steal from you?" Brother Thomas asked.

"He stole five grams from me," Derek said.

"When was this?" Brother Thomas asked.

"It was right after Thanksgiving," Derek said.

"Do you know why he stole it from you?" Brother Thomas asked.

"He yelled at me about having it. He's been on my case since I got here. I don't see how he gets to tell me how to live my life. I'm paying my own rent," Derek said.

"So he did it to help you go clean?" Brother Thomas asked.

"Yeah, and I had to wait like a week to get more," Derek said. He added a few disapprobative, but surprisingly creative, names for his cousin.

"What were the five grams contained in?" Brother Thomas asked.

"What do you mean?" Derek asked.

"Was it on something that might have gotten heroin on Frank? Or especially on whatever pocket he stuck it in?" Brother Thomas asked.

"I don't know," Derek said in a voice that indicated his apathy was in equal measure to his ignorance.

"The problem is that Frank did something with the heroin. Something quite illegal. If we can't find traces of the heroin on his clothes, then you're going to have to testify in court that he took it. I presume you'd make up a story about giving some homeless guy a place to sleep for the night and how Frank took it off of him. Though of course honesty would be closer to perfection," Brother Thomas said.

Derek turned a shade paler.

"I think it was in a plastic bag," he said.

"That's unfortunate, but you never know for sure. Did he put it into a pocket?" Brother Thomas asked.

Derek stared at a part of the room which Brother Thomas correctly guessed was where Frank had been standing when he had found and taken away the heroin.

"I think..." he said, but it trailed off. It is a measure of how intensely focused Brother Thomas was that he was not even *tempted* to make a joke in response.

"I think he put it in his coat. One of the pockets," Derek

said, and patted his own belly to indicate which pocket.

"Is that good enough?" he asked.

"We can hope," Brother Thomas said. "It is better his coat than his pants, since the pants would have certainly been washed by now. Still, I can promise nothing; the heroin would have had to get outside of the plastic bag to leave traces on his coat."

"You better not say anything about me to the cops," Derek said.

"If I have to tell the police about you, I would only say that you told me you knew how Frank got the heroin. I would leave it to you to be honest or lie to protect yourself as you chose," Brother Thomas said.

"Try not to," Derek said.

"I will do my best," Brother Thomas said.

He looked around the room.

"Have you considered a treatment program?" Sonia asked Derek.

"No. I don't want to stop," Derek said.

"Why not?" Sonia asked.

"Because when I do H, it's how I'm supposed to feel. I just wish that I could do it more often," he said.

"Aren't you afraid of losing your job?" Sonia asked.

"No," Derek said.

"Many users of recreational drugs, even sometimes heavy stuff, manage to keep their lives relatively intact. Of course, many also utterly destroy their lives. Heroin is especially dangerous because it feels so good that it becomes harder and harder to care about anything in real life. That makes holding down a job very difficult, but it's not, strictly speaking, impossible," Brother Thomas said.

"Are you actually supporting using heroin?" Sonia asked.

"Not at all. Heroin is a terrible idea because it destroys your ability to appreciate real life. For example: Derek, how beautiful is the snow?"

"I hate the snow," Derek said.

"How about a tree?"

"I don't like trees," Derek said.

"How beautiful is a sunset?" Brother Thomas asked.

"Sunsets are for losers," Derek said.

"Heard any good music lately?" Brother Thomas asked.

Derek analogized modern music to a traditional garden fertilizer often provided by domestic animals.

"How pretty is Sonia?" he asked.

"Whatever," Derek said.

"Is there anything in the world that's good besides heroin?" Brother Thomas asked him.

"No, not really," Derek said disdainfully.

"And that's the problem with heroin," Brother Thomas said to Sonia.

"Are you making fun of me?" Derek asked.

"No, I'm simply using you as an illustration to answer Sonia's question. The real reason to not use heroin is that it destroys your ability to appreciate real life. Miserable people can hold down a job, so if one is going to advocate for sobriety, it's best to do it for reasons that are true. Or rather, for reasons that are always true," Brother Thomas said.

"Dude, I don't care," Derek said.

"Neither do I. It's your life to throw away, and was there really anything to your life worth keeping? Was there anything that you were any good at?" Brother Thomas asked.

"Actually, I could draw," Derek said.

"Well, Okay, but was there anything you liked before you started using heroin?" he asked.

Derek thought about it.

"I liked drawing," he said. "I was going to draw comics when I grew up."

Derek paused, caught in reflection. He seemed to forget that his guests were there, and after a minute, a tear ran down his cheek.

Brother Thomas motioned to Brother Francis and Sonia, and they silently left the room, closed the door, went down the stairs and out onto the street.

"That was amazing," Sonia said.

"What? That I made an addict cry?" Brother Thomas asked. He seemed to be giving Sonia about half his attention, the other half presumably being on their next step.

"That you got him to realize what he's lost," Sonia said.

"That's overstating it," Brother Thomas said.

"Do you think he might try to quit?" Sonia asked.

"What? Because of what I said? No. Not with heroin. The addiction is incredibly powerful. If I did anything of any lasting significance, and frankly I doubt that I did, it was just to push him towards total breakdown a little faster. Which is not nothing, but it's a very small drop in the bucket of what he needs," Brother Thomas said.

"Did you mean the rest of what you said? I mean, about addicts being able to hold jobs?" Sonia asked.

"Oh yes. Drug addiction does not guarantee that you will lose your job. It makes it far too likely, but it doesn't guarantee it. It does guarantee that a lot of your time and money is going to go to drugs, which are just a complete waste of time. That's the real sin. We have so little time compared to what we could do with it. To waste it on telling yourself pleasing chemical lies is like hitting a pause button on your life. What's the difference between living fully and dying young and spending most of your life not living and dying old? You have just as many real moments in both. Drugs are just a sort of temporary suicide which eventually add up to a more permanent one," Brother Thomas said.

"You really don't like drugs, do you?" Sonia asked.

"There is a tradition where suicides were buried at a cross-roads with a stake in their heart. It was the maximum disrespect that people could think of. Of course, there are often pathetic emotional excuses for suicide; and mental illness can drive people to it. That's as true of drugs as of outright suicide. Still, with that proviso, I take a very traditional view of any form of suicide. To throw your life away is the greatest mistake a man can make. You can love and pray for the man but it is an awful thing to condone the mistake. It's the opposite of loving the man, because condoning the mistake is saying that the man's life wasn't actually worth anything," Brother Thomas said.

"That was nearly verbatim to the last time I heard you explain why you hate drug abuse," Brother Francis observed.

"I didn't memorize it, I just tend to answer the same question the same way," Brother Thomas said.

"So what were you really thinking about?" Brother Francis asked.

"I was trying to figure out whether it would be worth it to try breaking into Frank Buskirk's home when he wasn't there."

"Is it?" Brother Francis asked.

"I don't think so. Our best course right now is to give everything that we have—which might be of use—to the sheriff. It should be enough for him to get a warrant. And going about it in the legally correct way will have the least risk of destroying the evidentiary value of what he can find without our help. I wish we knew what Buskirk did with Floden's diplomas, though," Brother Thomas said.

"There's a reasonable chance, I would think, that he burned them or used them as toilet paper," Brother Francis said.

"That would be unfortunate, from our perspective," Brother Thomas said.

"It would not be reasonable to expect him to make our lives easy," Brother Francis said.

"I do not expect it, but it is quite permissible to hope for things that you have no right to expect," Brother Thomas said.

He stared off into the distance, considering.

"Let us go to the police station and see if we can find the sheriff," he said,

Being already in town, they didn't have a long walk, and got to the police station six minutes later. Unfortunately, the sheriff had the day off. And for entirely understandable reasons, the department policy forbade giving out his home address. With some reluctance, the officer manning the station was persuaded to call the sheriff at home. He was there, and said that he would come to the station in about twenty minutes.

Waiting in a police station is never pleasant, even when you're there for virtuous reasons. The time passed, however, and the sheriff turned out to have given a very accurate estimate of when he would be in. Having guessed that he might be there to receive actionable information, he showed up in full uniform. He gestured for them to follow him into his office.

"Good afternoon," he said.

"Good afternoon, Sheriff," Brother Thomas said.

"You have evidence for me?" he asked.

"Indeed we do. It's not enough to create an airtight case, unfortunately, but outside of a courtroom it is pretty conclusive. We can hope that with your forensic powers, you can find enough of the rest to plug any holes a defense lawyer could poke," Brother Thomas said.

He related the fight between Buskirk and Floden and the motive this created, and how they tracked down the needle. He gave the sheriff the stationery with the vet office's letterhead and the two names on it.

"I'll have to confirm this with the vet, of course, but that is very interesting. It's not quite conclusive proof, though. Someone could have taken the needles from Buskirk," the sheriff said.

"Someone could have, but that would make it a rather extraordinary coincidence that less than a month before the murder, he took five grams of heroin off of an addict," Brother Thomas said.

The Sheriff whistled.

"And you can prove it?"

"He has a cousin, living in town, who witnessed it. He's not the brightest light bulb in the silverware drawer, if you take my meaning, so he might not make the best witness in the witness box. But he saw Frank stuff the heroin into his—Frank's—coat pocket. Forensic analysis might find traces of it there. People rarely wash their winter coats," Brother Thomas said.

"It's worth a look, if we can get a warrant to do it. I'll need to talk with this cousin, but with his testimony plus tracing the needles to him, I think that won't be too hard," the sheriff said.

"If I may put a word of caution delicately: when you talk

with Derek Buskirk, you may get the impression that his life may not have been one of perfect blamelessness. The authority inhering to your position may well frighten him into silence. If you tread very lightly from the beginning of your acquaintance with him, he may prove more useful to you," Brother Thomas said.

The sheriff laughed.

"That may be the most diplomatic thing I've ever heard in my life. Don't worry, I won't make him think that we're coming after him. If he's the addict he saw his cousin take five grams of heroin off of, we'll be running into him sooner or later anyway. I just hope for nothing worse than breaking into a store to rob it. That's the part of this job I don't like. You have to use your judgment, and it's not good enough," he said.

"In one of St. Paul's letters, he describes God as 'he who accomplishes all things according to the intentions of his will.' I don't know if you believe in God, but either way it is a very accurate description, by contrast, of human beings. We accomplish nothing according to the intentions of our wills. All we can do is our best, and then trust. It has been said that the worst moment for an atheist is when he's grateful and has no one to thank. I suspect it is really when he realizes that he doesn't know what he's doing and must act in trust, and has no one to trust in. If you prefer, that he must act in hope, and has no reason to hope."

"I wouldn't know what the worst thing for an atheist is. I'm a Christian, myself," the sheriff said. "Do you have anything else for me?"

"Nothing as yet, unfortunately," Brother Thomas said.

"This might be enough. We can hope it is," the sheriff said with a twinkle in his eye. "I'm much obliged to you, but

I've got a bunch of phone calls and grunt work to do now. I'll let you know how it turns out," he added, pulling up the address book on his computer and picking up the phone.

"God be with you," Brother Thomas said as he left the office, Brother Francis and Sonia following behind him.

"You'd have thought he would be grateful," Sonia said, when they got outside.

"He was," Brother Thomas said.

"He didn't seem like it," Sonia said.

"He said he was much obliged," Brother Thomas said.

"He said the words, but he didn't sound like he meant them," Sonia said.

"He had a lot to think about, and while we have undoubtedly helped him considerably, he's still got most of the work to do to put together the *legal* case in a way that will hold up in court. Beyond reasonable doubt is a high standard to prove things to," Brother Thomas said.

"I still say he didn't sound like he meant it," Sonia said.

"Not everything is given to everyone. The sheriff may simply be not very good at sounding like he means what he says," Brother Thomas observed.

"I don't understand how it can be hard to sound like you mean what you're saying," Sonia said.

"I'm guessing you also don't understand how it can be hard to do calculus problems," Brother Thomas countered.

Sonia was going to protest that it was different, but realized before she spoke that she couldn't defend that and remained silent instead.

Brother Thomas gave a kind smile.

"I've met a lot of people in the years I've been a member of the order. I've found that no matter what it is, there's somebody who finds it difficult," he said, gently.

"Have you ever met someone who finds it difficult to admit they're wrong?" Sonia asked, then smiled back.

All three laughed.

When the laughter subsided, Sonia asked, almost hesitantly, "So... Is this it? Is the investigation over?"

Brother Thomas exhaled thoughtfully.

"I'm not content," he said. "This may be the best that we can do, but for some reason I can't explain, I think there's something else."

"Do you mean that we could be wrong, or just that there's more evidence that we haven't discovered yet?" Brother Francis asked.

"The latter," Brother Thomas said.

"Do you have any idea what it could be?" Brother Francis asked.

"I'm not sure," Brother Thomas said.

He considered for a minute.

"Do you still have the keys to Dean Floden's office?" he asked Sonia.

"Yes," she said.

"Let's go there and see if we can't retrace the steps of predator and prey," Brother Thomas said.

They walked quickly over to Marduk Hall and paused when they stood in front of it.

"Did he wait for Floden to come?" Brother Thomas asked, as much of himself as of anyone else.

"Which way is Dean Floden's house?" Brother Francis asked.

Brother Thomas pointed down the hill, though a bit to the side of the road, since it was not a straight shot.

"And would that road have been the most sensible way for him to have come?" Brother Francis asked.

"It depends on whether he drove or walked," Sonia said.

"Would Buskirk have known that?" Brother Francis asked.

"Probably. Most professors who can, live in that direction," Sonia said.

"I would suggest, then, that Dr. Buskirk would have hid behind those bushes," Brother Francis said, pointing at some bushes across the street.

Brother Thomas studied the bushes.

"So close, do you think?" he asked.

"It probably would have seemed farther during a blizzard. In fact, during a blizzard, I think it's actually pretty far from where Floden had to have passed. And Buskirk would want to make a positive identification," Brother Francis said.

"I would think that just going into the building would be plenty of identification," Brother Thomas said.

"Ordinarily, yes. But Buskirk is new at this, *and* he's on a hero's quest. If he murdered the wrong person, he wouldn't be a hero. And it would probably waste his one chance to kill Dean Floden," Brother Francis said.

Brother Thomas walked over and looked at the bush, and considered the idea.

"I think you're right. A few of the branches are broken on the far side. If he hid inside of the bush he would not be very visible at night, especially in a blizzard and from a distance," Brother Thomas said.

"Inside the bush? He was being very cautious then, and even a little predatory," Brother Francis said.

"So he sees Dean Floden come up," Brother Thomas said, pointing and following with his finger an imaginary Dean Floden walking along the path the real one took. When the imaginary dean got to the door, Brother Thomas considered.

"I can't imagine he followed a few steps behind, so he waited for Floden to shut the door," he said.

They walked up to the door, and Sonia unlocked it. Brother Thomas pulled it open slowly, until it was just possible to peer in.

"You can actually see inside pretty well from here," he said.

"He sees the lower floor is empty, and walks in."

They walked in, then walked up the stairs, quietly. The stairs were solidly built, if old, and did not squeak.

"This would be the worst part, I think. You can't really see the landing from here, and when you get to the top you might see Floden standing there, waiting for you," Brother Thomas said.

"I think that Floden went to his desk and waited there, so there wouldn't have been much danger of it. If you're going to confront a blackmailer, you probably want to be someplace that feels like you have authority," Brother Francis said.

They rounded the top of the stairs and walked over to the office.

"Do you think that Floden would have left it open, or closed it?" Brother Francis asked.

"Left it open. He was expecting someone who came to blackmail him, not to murder him," Brother Thomas said.

Sonia unlocked the door. They pushed it open. It was well oiled and did not squeak either.

"The building seemed to be on Dr. Buskirk's side," Brother Francis said, "At least in the sense of helping him achieve his immediate goals, poor fellow."

They walked in, and Brother Thomas mimed the motion of uncapping a syringe. He walked forward into the dean's room.

"The needle in the neck argues that he was behind Floden. It's very easy to protect your neck from the front, though your chest not nearly as much," Brother Thomas said.

He mimed stabbing someone in the neck, then did it again but this time throwing an arm around the other person first.

"Dr. Buskirk is slightly taller than Dean Floden was, and I think that throwing an arm around him to hold his arms down would have been more effective than not. The victim will be reacting to the wrong thing while you stab him in the neck, and it makes it much harder for him to just go with the thrust and keep it from entering the skin," he said.

"What then?" Brother Francis asked. "I don't think heroin would take effect literally instantly, and he'd have someone fighting for his life in his arms."

"Sonia, could the desk lamp have been over here? You did say you thought it had been moved," Brother Thomas asked, pointing towards the closer side of the desk to where he stood.

"Yes," she said.

Brother Thomas mimed letting go with his right hand and picking up the lamp, then letting go to give himself enough space while hitting his imaginary victim on the back of the head with the heavy base of the lamp.

"That probably wouldn't incapacitate him, but it wouldn't have to stun him for long. Let's say that he had mostly filled the needles, and so injected two grams of heroin into Floden. Assuming that he was good or lucky in his aim, Floden would start to feel weird quickly. Even if hitting him on the head only bought Buskirk a few seconds, that would probably be enough. He could take a few steps back, and let Floden chase him around the desk waiting for the heroin to kick in,"

Brother Thomas said.

"Why the second injection, then?" Sonia asked.

"Thoroughness," Brother Thomas said.

"Both practical and moral—such as it was—thoroughness. Like they said in *The Usual Suspects*, if you're going to shoot the devil in the back, you better make sure that you don't miss," Brother Francis said.

"And why the arm? Injecting him in the neck in the first place would rule out suicide," Sonia said.

"I think it was a show of power. The veins in your arm are very easy to protect—as any nurse will tell you, they can be hard to find even with cooperation—so to do that to someone who was unwilling shows how completely you control them," Brother Francis said.

Sonia shivered.

"Do you think that the needle cap was found all the way over there because Buskirk was nervous?" Brother Thomas asked, pointing at the chair under which it was found.

Brother Francis nodded.

"So next he positions the body on the desk," Brother Thomas said.

"Why?" Sonia asked.

"I'm not sure. Either it was symbolic—he died where he did his evil—or it was just something random to try to confuse the police. Once his goal was achieved, or at least certain, I think he'd switch from being an avenging angel to being a hunted criminal trying to save himself. Not that it would be a complete switch, but I think that after he was successful, self-preservation would start to be his primary concern," Brother Francis said.

"Whatever the reason, he's put Floden on the desk. Next, I think, he gathers up the needles," Brother Thomas said.

"But leaves the caps?" Brother Francis asked.

"Assuming he wasn't stupid enough to put his saliva on them, they have no evidentiary value," Brother Thomas said.

"Then he throws them out the window for some reason," Brother Francis said.

"Perhaps he thought he heard something outside the office. If he's nervous, and now terrified that he's going to be caught, he might be jumpy. Say he hears something, or thinks that he does, and looks out of the window, sees the bush and no one around, and throws the needles down into it. Maybe he thinks that he's going to get them again later to dispose of them properly," Brother Thomas said. "Then what?"

"I think he would have come over here by the door and looked to see if anyone came in," Brother Francis said. "If someone did, he could walk to Floden and pretend that he just came in himself. If they just looked in, they wouldn't see him, and might not see the corpse."

"Then when no one comes he goes and looks out into the hallway?" Brother Thomas asked.

"And when he sees no one there, he goes down the stairs and checks," Brother Francis said.

"Then curses himself for a fool when he realizes the building is empty. So he goes back to finish making sure he left no traces, and that's when he sees the diplomas. They would have been framed, as the hooks on the wall testify," Brother Thomas said.

"About this big?" Brother Francis asked, holding his hands to two opposite corners of a rectangle the size of a diploma. "He could have hidden that in his coat."

"So then he leaves," Brother Thomas said.

They walked out of the office, Sonia locking the doors behind them. They went down the stairs and outside, again remembering to lock the doors.

"Now where did he go?" Brother Thomas asked.

They looked around.

"Do you think that he went home?" he asked.

"Maybe," Brother Francis said.

They all looked around again, trying to put themselves there that night, as someone newly a murderer.

"Or he might have reconsidered carrying the diplomas," Brother Francis said. "How far away is the psychology building?"

"It's right over there," Sonia said, pointing at a building about five hundred feet away.

"If he knew or had reason to believe that no one was in the building, he might have gone to his office," Brother Francis said. "Home would be a long trek with some bulky items under his coat he'd have to hold on to the whole time. A two-minute walk to hide the evidence he was holding might seem a lot wiser than a twenty-minute walk home."

"Isn't an office riskier than his own home?" Sonia asked.

"If he's not suspected, probably not," Brother Thomas said. "How many people go through other people's filing cabinets? And if he did this, he could, at his leisure, bring something into the office which would make smuggling the diplomas home safe and easy. But there again we come up against the unpleasant fact that he's had that leisure already."

"Yes, but to have and to use are two different things. It's early days yet, and when we met Dr. Buskirk, did he seem calm, collected, and calculating?" Brother Francis asked.

"True. And I am always too inclined to assume people are acting with rational self-control. The man we met might well have been hiding out at his house the entire time. He wanted us gone almost like an animal might chase something away from its burrow," Brother Thomas said.

"I think that it's likely enough that it's worth the time to take a look," Brother Francis said.

"I'm not suggesting that we leave stones unturned. Sonia, can you get the provost's home phone number?" Brother Thomas asked.

Sonia was able to get the number, and they tried it, but the Provost was not at home. After a bit of trying to track her down, they discovered that she was in her office, taking advantage of the holiday to get work done when no one would interrupt her. They decided to walk to her office to speak to her in person.

"Good afternoon. What may I do for you?" she asked as they walked into her office.

"Good afternoon. We're sorry to be bothering you on your day off," Brother Thomas said.

"That's okay. Truth be told, this only works half of the time anyway," the provost said.

"We need your help to search one of the professor's offices," Brother Thomas said.

"Which one?" she asked.

"Dr. Frank Buskirk's," Brother Thomas said.

"That would be easy enough to arrange," the provost said. "May I ask why?"

"There might be additional evidence that he killed Dean Floden there, which he has not yet removed," Brother Thomas said.

"Additional evidence?" she asked.

"We've found strong evidence that it was Dr. Buskirk who killed Dean Floden. The police are officially collecting it now. However, as I think you'll agree, it's best for everyone if the evidence can be as solid as possible. A trial which ends in acquittal but leaves everyone convinced that a guilty man got off would be... suboptimal," he said.

"Yes. If we have to go through a trial, better it be quick and obvious and give us cause to fire him. You can't imagine how difficult it is to get rid of tenured professors," she said.

"Isn't that the point of tenure?" Sonia asked.

"Tenure is an antiquated concept which serves no place in a modern university," the provost said.

Perceiving Sonia to be a bit shocked, she explained.

"Tenure used to mean that once you knew someone wasn't an idiot, they could have the freedom to pursue truth rigorously. Now it means that once they've jumped through enough hoops and are good enough at conforming, they don't have to publish or care about students or do anything else to help the university."

This did not have the hoped-for effect, but the provost had reached the limits of how much she cared, so she did not explain any further.

"From whom can we get the keys?" asked Brother Thomas, refusing to get distracted by side issues.

"Ordinarily I would ask the maintenance staff to let you in, but they have the day off, with someone on call for emergencies. I don't think that this qualifies, so I'll go get them from the safe where we keep the master keys."

She finished typing something she had been working on, locked her computer, then rose and walked out of the room. She returned about three minutes later.

"Here are the keys to the front door and to Dr. Buskirk's office. Please don't lose them, as it will be a pain to get copies made if you do," she said, handing them to Brother Thomas.

"Thank you, and we will return both promptly," he said.

They took their leave and went directly to the psychology

building. As they expected, it was locked and empty. They went as directly to Dr. Buskirk's office as having to follow the signs indicating the layout of office numbers would permit.

Dr. Buskirk's office was not spacious, but neither was it tiny. Judging by professional standards, he kept it neat. As they looked around, Brother Francis noticed some framed diplomas hung on the wall.

"Wouldn't it be funny if he just hung them in his own office on the grounds that no one ever reads framed diplomas?" Brother Francis asked.

He moved closer and examined them, but they belonged to Dr. Buskirk. They split up and began to examine the room more thoroughly. As Sonia's perusing through a filing cabinet was turning up nothing, she looked over to see Brother Thomas who was, to her surprise, freely handling Dr. Buskirk's desk.

"You're not worried about smudging fingerprints?" she asked.

"We don't need to prove that Dr. Buskirk has been in his own office," Brother Thomas said.

Sonia laughed.

"Sorry, that was a dumb question," she said.

"You're just not used to investigating. The novelty of it makes you think of how you've seen it done, probably on television," Brother Thomas said, somewhat absentmindedly.

"But I thought that this is the first murder you've investigated," Sonia said.

"It is, but we've investigated other things where fingerprints were evidence. Industrial espionage, fraud, theft—that sort of thing," Brother Thomas said.

Sonia nodded and got back to work.

"I'm not finding anything," she said after some time.

"Nor am I, but there's still plenty left to search through," Brother Thomas said.

Sonia had finished examining every possible place and several impossible places inside of the filing cabinets. She was about to move on to something else when she realized that she hadn't looked behind them. In a moment she was glad that she did. Behind the cabinets were a pair of objects which looked like frames.

She used her cell phone as a flashlight and was fairly sure that the things were in fact frames. She tried to reach behind the cabinets, and while her fingers could touch them, she was not able to get any purchase on them to pull them out.

"Brother Thomas," she called.

"Yes?" he said.

"I think I may have found them—I found something framed, at any rate—back behind this filing cabinet, but my arm isn't long enough to pull them out," she said.

He came over and, after she pointed them out, he reached and was able to get them to move. When the first one came out, the shining seal of some sort of official document glinted in the light, and a few moments' perusal proved it to be Dean Floden's doctoral diploma.

"Should we put it back?" Brother Francis asked.

"As tempting as that might be, everything should be as upfront as possible. The exact position has no evidentiary value, and all three of us can testify where it was, approximately. Let's leave it here, turn off the lights, lock the door, call the sheriff, and wait outside the office," he said.

The sheriff had returned to the police station only a few minutes before their call, and left immediately upon receiving it.

"Sonia, would you mind calling the provost at her office?

As the sheriff has not yet obtained a warrant to search Dr. Buskirk's house and office, he will need her permission to search here. Since the office is the university's property, her permission will be sufficient," Brother Thomas said.

Sonia placed the call and made the request. The provost turned up less than a minute after the sheriff, so there was no great amount of waiting. With the provost's permission and in the sheriff's presence, they opened the door again, and showed him what they had found. The sheriff fished out the other framed object, which turned out to be the dean's undergraduate diploma.

The sheriff whistled.

"With this too, I can't imagine I'll have any trouble with the warrant request," he said, then he furrowed his brows.

"It wasn't very smart of him to bring the degrees here, was it?"

"Or to take them in the first place," Sonia added.

"I can think of no cases in which murdering someone could be described as 'very smart'. I don't think we can be too surprised if the actions surrounding the murder are no greater acts of genius than the murder itself," Brother Thomas said.

"True enough," the sheriff agreed. "The ordinary criminals we deal with do all sorts of unbelievably stupid things. There've been more than a few cases where someone posted all the evidence we needed to convict them on Facebook."

"Will you need anything further of me?" the provost asked the sheriff.

"No, ma'am," he said.

She waved farewell and left.

"Well, I'm quite grateful to you for all the help you've given me," the sheriff said to the brothers.

"It's our pleasure," Brother Thomas said. "I hope that what we've given you so far plus what you'll find at Dr. Buskirk's house will be enough to convict. Either way, I doubt that we will be able to supply you with any further evidence, so I suspect that this is goodbye. At least until the trial, if there is one."

The sheriff extended his hand, and Brother Thomas shook it. The sheriff in turn shook Brother Francis's hand and Sonia's hand.

The four left the building together. Sonia locked it, then after bidding farewell to the sheriff, she and the brothers went to the administration building where they returned the keys to the provost.

"Before you go," she said to them, "I don't really care what the evidence against Dr. Buskirk is, but do you know why he did it?"

Brother Thomas explained about the grant, and Dean Floden's leading Dr. Buskirk on while actually sabotaging him. When the recital was finished, the provost exhaled deeply.

"Jack was a piece of work. If we were in Texas, Dr. Buskirk might be able to get away with the he-had-it-coming-to-him defense. In a sense, I think he did us a favor," she said.

"In a sense, he did. But I don't think the same sense that you meant. It's true that you're fortunate to be rid of Jack Floden, but you could have done that yourself. I think that the real favor that Frank Buskirk did was to show you how bad this place has gotten," Brother Thomas said.

To the provost, this came almost like a blow. She grunted in pained recognition of an ugly truth.

"I hope that you will forgive me for saying it, but this is the danger of putting the good of an institution above the good the institution was created to do. Staci Blender-more said the other night that universities are like giant oak trees—they keep growing according to their nature, and the wind sometimes pushes the leaves around, but they come back to where they're supposed to be; perhaps every now and then the wind breaks a branch, but you'd never know it to look at the tree from the ground. She's right. Whatever you tolerate for the greater good—whether it's sexual harassment or English departments teaching bad politics and terrible philosophy instead of English—whatever good you get from not ruffling feathers doesn't matter in the long term. What you lose is the reason there's a university at all.

"If you'll pardon me for telling you your own business, Staci is a smart woman. She doesn't flaunt it, but she's no fool. You could do a lot worse than to make sure she's on the search committee for picking out the next dean. If you can't get her to be the dean outright, I mean."

"I'll think about it," the provost said.

"I'm not going to tell anyone else about the suggestion. You're quite free to do whatever you want with it. If nothing else, you might want to just have lunch with her. She's a person worth talking to. So is her husband, though for other reasons, since he's so removed from the day-to-day life of the university," Brother Thomas said.

"I will certainly have lunch with her. I've seen enough of you to know that you know people. And if nothing else, I owe you for clearing this mess up," she said, and smiled.

Brother Thomas smiled back.

"God be with you," he said, and left, Brother Francis and Sonia silently following.

* * *

When they got outside, Brother Thomas was the first one to speak.

"There are some things I need to do alone, since we'll be leaving tomorrow. You two go to dinner and I'll catch up if I can. If not, don't worry, we won't leave tomorrow without saying goodbye," he said.

Neither Sonia nor Brother Francis protested, and they walked off in the direction of President Blendermore's house. There were two people Brother Thomas intended to talk with, and he wondered which he should see first. After a little consideration, he decided to go with the easier one, as it would mostly likely take only a little time and then he would be guaranteed to see both.

Accordingly, he set off toward Tiffany's house.

* * *

It was a small house in what was clearly not the best part of town, but it was still a house and in decent repair. Brother Thomas knocked on the door. A minute later, Tiffany opened it.

"What are you doing here?" she asked. She was merely surprised, and not unfriendly.

"I want to let you know that the police have their suspect and a pretty strong case against him, so your helping us was indeed in your interest," Brother Thomas said.

"Really? Want to come in?" she said.

"Just for a moment. I don't have much to say," he said.

He walked in, but didn't take off his cloak, and accordingly Tiffany didn't bother closing the front door after the storm door.

"I wanted to let you know that what I said wasn't a bluff. I wasn't trying to deceive you, I really was just trying to put things as clearly as I could," Brother Thomas said.

"I knew that," she said.

She looked a little sheepish.

"Truth to tell, I knew that then, too. I don't regret what I did, but I'm not proud of it, either, and I didn't want anyone prying into it or talking about it."

"No one ever wants that," Brother Thomas said.

"I suppose you'd say it's because the truth can be painful," she said.

"I'd only say it if you didn't know it already," he said.

"I really can't tell if you're judging me or not," she said.

"I don't judge. There's no point. What's confusing you is that most people need to pretend that everything a person does is good in order to value them. But a person is lovable for the good they can do, not for the good they have already done or the evil that they haven't."

"But what if they're not going to do that good?" she asked.

"If it could be guaranteed that they won't do it, then strictly speaking it's not good that they can do. But there are few guarantees in this world, and none when it comes to the choices that people will make. Having said that, there's no sense in wanting people to love an illusion of you instead of you."

"They might treat you better," she said.

"And you'll spend every moment wondering when it will all fall apart. Build your life around an illusion, and not only will you not enjoy the things you got from it, you won't even enjoy the things that you would have gotten anyway. When the illusion falls apart, the collapse will take everything," he said.

Tiffany was silent, but she was considering, not cowed.

"If I may suggest it, you're in a unique position to experiment and find out which you prefer. Sonia knows the secrets you've been keeping, or at least all the worst ones. Whatever friendship you could build up with her would have to be real."

"What if she won't have me as a friend?"

"Then *you* would know something about *Sonia*. Living your life based on illusions about others will make you just as unhappy as living it based on others' illusions about you. Sonia learned that recently, as her illusions about this place have been torn down. You may have more in common that you think, having until now been flip sides of the same coin. You held up an illusion. She wanted to believe it. Perhaps you can find common ground in learning to live with the truth," he said.

"Are you sure that you're a detective and not a counselor?" she asked.

"They're the same thing. People go to counselors because they're trapped by something. The truth will set you free, and the only way to learn the truth is to find it out. And if you think that sounds rehearsed, ask Sonia about that."

He smiled, though whether more to himself or to her wasn't clear.

"I'd wish you good luck, but luck is just a name for what we don't understand. God be with you," he said.

Tiffany chuckled.

He nodded in farewell and left. She closed the door very thoughtfully after him.

He walked out to the street then pulled out his phone and looked at the map. The easy one over, it was time to tackle the difficult one.

* * *

Dr. Deborah Marten's house was larger and better-located than Tiffany's was. He walked up to the door, and finding a knocker on it, used that in preference to the door bell. She opened it not long after, but froze when she saw who it was. She started to close the door, but checked herself.

"What the hell do you want?" she demanded.

"Interesting choice of words. There are a few things that I wanted to tell you which might make your life easier," he said.

"What?" she said, her hostility unabated.

"First, I'm assuming you don't know what killed Dean Floden, and without disclosing that, it wasn't the rat poison you had Paresh put in his rum."

She was about to protest but he cut her off with both word and gesture.

"Stop. This isn't a trick. Don't bother confirming or denying any of what I say, just hear me out. He never, so far as I know, drank from the bottle after Paresh put the cut-up rat poison into it. There were several things wrong with that plan, so it never would have worked, by the way. Rat poison might be odorless and tasteless, but rat bait is anything but. After all, there has to be some reason for the rat to eat it. And it's also generally water resistant, so it didn't dissolve into the rum. Floden would have had to have been dead drunk before he might have swallowed any. Plus the dosage in rat bait is too low for a full-grown human. So while you might be guilty of attempted murder, there's no way you'd ever have been guilty of successful murder."

She opened her mouth to say something, but couldn't

decide what. He held up his hand to stop her, and said, "Just wait a little more. I'll be done soon."

"I haven't told any of this to the police, and I don't intend to. For one thing, while I could prove it—the clerk at the Ace Hardware recognized the picture of you I texted him—I really doubt that the DA would prosecute. It's not that no harm no foul is the law, but human laziness is on your side. For another, most of the consequences would fall on Paresh, which was, after all, your plan if things went wrong. And I don't think that there's anything to be gained by sending him to prison—he's not going to make this mistake again.

"Which brings us to you. There are two ways I see this going. One is that you're really just a monster, at this point, and not getting caught emboldens you. But everything falling on Paresh would embolden you too. The other possibility is that there's some humanity still left in you, and you're horrified about how you nearly murdered one human being and manipulated someone who trusted you into doing it to his tremendous risk.

"I believe that it's the latter, which is why you're being so defensive. It's a terrible strategy, and if you actually had ice water in your veins, you wouldn't use it. I think you're being defensive as a way of protecting yourself from yourself. You hate me because I remind you of what you've done, and you're trying desperately not to think about it."

Dr. Marten's expression had gradually shifted to neutral. At these last words, she looked sad.

"It doesn't matter how you got here. It would be useful for you to figure out, but it's largely academic. The question which matters is how you get out of here. And you can. You are not, in your essence, a murderer. No human being is. But you've been given an unusual gift. You've seen just how bad it's possible to become. It's a bit like the inverse of what George Bailey gets in It's a Wonderful Life.

"But here's the thing: reclaiming yourself is not a trick. I can summarize it very briefly as 'be as good as you possibly can be,' but when one has gone as far down the rabbit hole as you have, I don't think that's going to mean much. You can't change *one* thing, you have to change *everything*. That's a process, and what you need is a friend to help you through it."

He handed her one of his cards with a name and number written on the back of it.

"She's a professor of philosophy. One good place to start in overhauling your life is your scholarship. You call it literary criticism, but where it isn't just complaining, it's fifth-rate philosophy. If you want to be a nihilist, go ahead, but at least learn what you're talking about. Sarah Gallager is quite knowledgeable in her field. Working with her to learn some decent philosophy would be a good excuse to become friends. And you'd do very well to have her as a friend. She's a good person.

"And yes, what I'm saying is very harsh. I'm leaving tomorrow and I don't have the time to be gentle. Right now, you are mostly dead. The good news is that you can come back to life. You can become a great person. But you can also get worse. So, if you can, forget about me. I don't matter at all. Go make a friend who has some theory of happiness that can actually work. The nice thing about happy people is that they want to give it away.

"And if you do manage to become a decent person, help out Paresh. You owe him a great deal for what you've done to him.

"Good night, and God be with you."

Without waiting for a reply, he turned and left. She watched him go, a maelstrom of emotions effectively paralyzing her for some time. When he was out of sight, she crumpled to the ground in a heap and quietly cried. At last the cold made it too uncomfortable to stay where she was and she got up, closed the door and went inside to think.

* * *

Brother Thomas made it to President Blendermore's house in time to catch the end of dinner.

"So what were you up to?" Sonia asked.

"He was talking to the people we've met and telling them where to get help," Brother Francis said.

"Once an investigation is over, it becomes practical to burn your bridges," Brother Thomas said.

"How is telling someone where to get help burning your bridges? Doesn't helping someone usually make them grateful to you?" Sonia said.

"I see this hasn't come up very often in your life," Brother Thomas said, though it was with a smile.

"I've helped a few people," Sonia said.

"Who didn't ask for it?" Brother Thomas asked.

"Well, no. They did ask for it," Sonia said.

"There are few things less forgivable than unsolicited advice. Especially unsolicited advice which is right," Brother Thomas said.

"Then why give it?" Sonia asked.

"Because it might help," Brother Thomas said.

"I really should have seen that coming," Sonia said.

"You should have," Brother Thomas agreed.

* * *

The next morning, Sonia came over to the president's house early enough that Brother Thomas almost wondered if she didn't trust him to track her down before they left. Ian and Staci together made a breakfast that was a creditable counterpoint to the one Michael had made, then bid farewell to the detectives.

Sonia walked them to their car, and even helped them scrape off the ice and snow which had accumulated during their stay.

Finally it came time to say goodbye.

"I'm really going to miss you guys," she said. "I know we've only spent a few days together, but it's been pretty intense, and absolutely fascinating."

"It's been a pleasure having your help," Brother Thomas said.

"And also interesting to get the opportunity to see the university through your eyes," Brother Francis added.

"Would it be okay if I took Michael up on that invitation to come visit?" Sonia asked.

"You'd be most welcome," Brother Thomas said.

"Please do. As you might imagine, our travel budget is limited," Brother Francis said.

Impulsively, Sonia hugged each of them in turn, then stood back as they got in the car and pulled out. She waved goodbye until she couldn't see them any more.

When they were out of view, she took a deep breath, and took stock. It was sad that the exciting times were over, but there was also an element of relief. Excitement can be tiring, and it would be nice to get back to life as normal. Except that it wasn't normal anymore. The university in which she got her degree and in which she had worked since then had changed. Of course, it was actually the same university, she just knew more about it. Her relationship to it certainly had to change.

Her phone beeped. It was a text from Tiffany.

"Want to have lunch?" it read.

Sonia thought about it. Everything she had learned about Tiffany made her hesitate. How could she not be miserably uncomfortable around Tiffany? But then, of whom would that not be true? If they weren't someone she had learned something about, there was the question of what it was she didn't know. And even if they were what they seemed, there would now be the gulf of what she knew about the rest of the university...

She took another deep breath, and texted back, "Sure."

It was as a good a place as any to start getting used to the university as it really was.

* * *

When the brothers had returned to their house and brought their little luggage in, Brother Thomas went to see Brother Wolfgang to tell him the results.

When Brother Thomas entered Brother Wolfgang's office, he looked up and asked, "Well?"

"I believe so," Brother Thomas said.

"Tell me," Brother Wolfgang said.

And he told him, with enough detail to make things as they stood intelligible.

"And did you find it as exciting as you expected?" Brother Wolfgang asked.

"Indeed I did," Brother Thomas said.

"When you left, I expected to tell you on your return that it was not a very important case, since there was nothing to repair. Yet it seems that you did find relationships to repair, if mostly relationships which should have existed but didn't. Let us pray that you were successful."

"Let us indeed," Brother Thomas said.

"And do you think that Brother Francis found it as exciting as you did?" Brother Wolfgang asked.

"I doubt it, since he seems more normal than me. But certainly he did enjoy himself," Brother Thomas said.

"That's well for him, then. This morning, before you got back, I received a request from the Archbishop of Philadelphia to look into the death of a wealthy businessman," Brother Wolfgang said.

"Who died under mysterious circumstances?" Brother Thomas asked.

Brother Wolfgang smiled.

"Exceedingly."

Author's Note

I hope that you enjoyed The Dean Died On Winter Break. If you did, I apologize that it wasn't longer—in stories that we like, we come to care about the characters, and they have life more or less in proportion to page count. On the other hand their quality of life is defined by the quality of those pages, which in large part forms the practical limitation that keeps novels from being millions of pages long. But certainly had I been a better writer, I could have written more, not only at the same quality, but better, and though I did my best, there is no one to whom it is more apparent than me that my best falls painfully short. If you wanted more, so did I, and you have my sympathy. (If you didn't like it but read this far anyway, I think that the person you should really blame is not me, but whoever it was that made you read what you would rather not.)

The Dean Died On Winter Break began life as a novel called "A Murder at Yalevard" and featured two consulting detectives, Peter and Felicia, who had independently been hired to look into the murder of one of the deans, and after suspecting each other, teamed up. Stated that generally, it's not a bad premise, but I just didn't like the detectives. At the time, I had been trying to avoid characters that had anything in common with me for fear of having them called author self-inserts. This was especially unfortunate because I have a deeply inquisitive nature and find almost everything interesting; the result was characters without interests and consequently without personality (the easiest way to know personality is by what people find interesting). A better writer than I might perhaps be able to make bland characters interesting, but it is in any event beyond my skill, and the story languished while I wrote others. In the wake of disliking these detectives, I stopped worrying about who my characters might be accused of resembling and focused on the simple question of what characters would I like to read about? After several novels I was happy with, I got to thinking about the murder mysteries I had written (I also wrote a draft of a sequel about a murdered law professor, titled A Good Start), and I concluded that the mysteries themselves were good, the detectives were the only insuperable problem.

Then I thought about the detective stories I like to read: Cadfael, Lord Peter Wimsey, Father Brown, Poirot, Sherlock Holmes, and also as the ones I like to watch: Murder She Wrote, Scooby Doo Where Are You?, Murder in Paradise. Of these, my favorite stories to read are the Chronicles of Brother Cadfael. Though good, they're not necessarily the best mysteries, but they are the ones I keep coming back to more than the others. Part of this is the setting. Ellis Peters paints a wonderfully enticing picture of medieval England, full of fascinating characters, and it's a place I like to spend time, if only in the imagination shared between author and reader. But there is a flaw in the Cadfael stories, which runs more or less through the heart of them: Cadfael's vocation as a detective is at odds with his vocation as a monk. Our modern world knows friars better than it does monks, though neither very well. Much of the point of the Benedictines was to create little pockets of a better world within a larger world filled with evils. They created fortresses in which it was possible to be holy, that there might be holiness somewhere on earth. And when the wider world was physically dangerous, these holy spaces doubled as safe spaces—the Benedictines were the first great hoteliers, and people would travel Europe from abbey to abbey because they could be sure of finding safe lodging.

To this end, the Benedictines took a vow of stability, in addition to the vows of poverty, chastity, and obedience which all consecrated religious take. Monks promise to stay in their abbey. It's not an absolute promise of staying inside the walls of the abbey, of course—it's a vow of stability, not immobility—but it is meant as a division of labor, where the monk will tend his garden and leave the outside world to tend itself. The outside world often does so bad a job at it that if the monk doesn't tend his garden, nowhere at all will be tended. Human beings are finite creatures, and to pretend that we can fix the whole world is mostly to ensure that we will fix nothing at all.

And this is the problem with the Cadfael stories. The murders happen almost entirely outside of the Abbey of Saint Peter and Saint Paul, where Cadfael has vowed to be stable. Granted, the murder investigations are the exception to his normal stability, but he clearly feels the tension. Now, there is nothing inherently wrong with tension. As the modern world has largely forgotten about marriage, the whole reason to make a vow is because you might want to break it. No one vows that a hacksaw shall never shave his beard, or to never slap himself in the face with a salmon six hundred and thirty seven times a day. There is no point in vowing to *not* do what you would never do anyway. Vows only exist to prevent you from doing what you *would* do if it were not for the vow. But in the Cadfael stories, more than occasionally to be a good detective he is a bad monk. My point is liable to be misunderstood, so I'd like to be clear that to be a bad monk is not necessarily to be a bad man, especially in the sense that most men are not meant to be monks and so most of us are supposed to have other virtues than the monastic ones. But because we who are still in the world are not supposed to have the specially monastic virtues, it does not follow that monks shouldn't have them either.

The Chronicles of Brother Cadfael are, therefore, the stories of when Brother Cadfael is *least* a monk. All novels are set in unusual times in the main characters' lives, but the ideal is that it is at times when circumstances are exceptional that we'll be seeing the characters when they are *most* themselves. If we are seeing Cadfael when he is most himself, then he is not really a monk. I have no doubt that many people would enjoy that, because many people like to identify with the main character of a story, and most people are not monks. But *I* don't find fundamental confusion about life to be appealing in a main character. I'm much more interested in seeing people who have made peace with reality as it is, and are doing their best to make positive progress, rather than wrestling with undoing their major mistakes. I'm not saying that the latter is illegitimate, just that it's not what I most want to read. And to be clear, I love the Chronicles of Brother Cadfael, this is just something that keeps me from enjoying them as much as I could.

Considering other detectives, Father Brown showed how

well a priest can be a detective as his detection might well be part of his ministry. I have no doubt that there will be many priest-detectives in stories to come, but I'm also very fond of Scooby Doo, which I think shows that detectives are at their best when they're in community. Hence why I went with a friar as my detective. Like priests it is the vocation of friars to go out in the world, and but unlike priests it would be natural enough for a detective friar exist in a community of detectives, because friars can be dedicated to any good purpose which can't support a just wage for the workers.

Community is so important because it brings with it the idea of complementarity. There are two ways to show off virtue. The easiest and most common is to contrast it with vice, and from this comparison arises the mistaken belief that fictional characters must have flaws in order to be interesting. Virtues can also be shown off by comparison with other virtues, especially those which are hard to hold at the same time. It is not easy to be an expert in psychology and an expert in poisons and an expert in soil types and an expert in fashion. Human intellects being finite must be specialized, and the most interesting conversations are almost always when two experts in different fields talk to each other. And when this happens it is always dramatic, because it is never certain that either will understand the other. In an academic setting, no one much cares—nothing is at stake—but in a mystery the solution of the mystery is often dependent on whether the experts can communicate with each other, because the solution relies on the knowledge of both being inside the head of one.

Finally, I settled on a Franciscan order for several reasons, the most important of which is that a big part of the Franciscan charism is a love of the particular. That suits detection extremely well; in detective fiction the classic mistake of the hasty police officer is the not-actually-a-syllogism, "The killer must have had a motive, this man had a motive, therefore this man must be the killer." Though his logic is none too good, his real error is his generalism. He doesn't ask anything about the particular man who has the motive; he never thinks to ask whether the motive would be sufficient for *him*.

I was very pleased with the result, finding that it balanced out a number of virtues that could exist simultaneously but were not easy to hold in one person. I think that it will give a wide scope for showing off the detectives (and their friends) as they meet new people, and new approaches and new dynamics become required of them. We shall see, but at any rate I find the beginning encouraging, and will certainly try to see it through.

The question was brought to my attention of whether I intentionally omitted the scene where the killer finds out that he's been caught. The answer is yes. I would have found the scene too painful to read, so I didn't include it. But if you're curious, Buskirk was paralyzed with fear when he looked through the window and saw that it was the sheriff knocking on his door. He racked his brains for what to do, alternating between playing it cool and running, until the thought that if he was being arrested he'd never get away became too strong, and he ran out of his back door. He had a very short lead on his pursuers, tired quickly from sprinting in the snow, and was caught. When caught he basically crumpled into a heap from which he did not arise throughout his trial and afterwards being sent to prison. Please pray for those people who basically do the same thing, but are real.

A REQUEST FROM THE AUTHOR

Spreading the word of a novel to the people who would enjoy reading it is difficult under the most favorable of circumstances, and in the rare cases those do come about, it's usually long after the death of the author. Since as of the time of this writing I'm still alive, the most favorable of circumstances aren't even a consideration, and so I would be all the more appreciative for any help which you can give in spreading the word:

Tell your friends. If you know anyone who might enjoy reading this novel, it would be a kindness to both of us to tell them about it. Posting about it on social media is good too.

Review it on Amazon. Book reviews on amazon are helpful in a variety of ways. Having a large number of reviews is beneficial both to the book turning up in searches, as well as to just being reassuring to potential readers. Equally important is that informative reviews can catch a potential reader's eye. It's not so much a matter of whether the review is favorable or not, but whether it says what there is that might be worth reading, and to whom. A review of a sci-fi book which said, "It frequently goes into mind-numbing detail about the minutiae of space travel and NASA bureaucracy with a stubborn adherence to realism that leaves excitement far behind," would all but guarantee my friend Tom would read it.

Review it Anywhere. Any review is a big help. Reviews in prominent places are obviously great, but reviews on small blogs, in niche magazines, etc. are also very much appreciated.

Ask Your Local Library to Carry It. Public libraries often take reader recommendations seriously, though of course there are no guarantees. There are other libraries besides public libraries, too. Schools typically have libraries, and other clubs and organizations might as well.

ABOUT CHRISTOPHER LANSDOWN

In college I majored in math, computer science, and philosophy, though later downgraded philosophy to a minor when one of the professors told me that he thought people got too hung up over contradictions in arguments. I went on to get a master's degree in math, then found work as a professional programmer. I've picked up a variety of skills like dancing (mostly Lindy Hop), knitting, spinning wool, building spinning wheels, archery, making longbows, bow hunting for food, making and flying kites, bread making, pasta making (my favorite was pumpkin ravioli), and tailoring (mostly making pants for Lindy Hopping). To stay in shape I lift weights and go to an indoor rock climbing gym.

I wanted to be a novelist since around the time I first read a novel, and my interests in writing are as eclectic as my reading. I'm especially fond of interesting characters, but I maintain that what really makes a character interesting are his virtues, not his vices; vices are at best a way of highlighting virtues, and I think that they're often used as a crutch. What really makes virtues interesting in fiction is when a character is tempted, and having the character give into that temptation is just an easy way of making the temptation seem real. Being detail oriented, I'm also very fond of plots which don't have plot holes, which is a lot of work to write, but I figure that if I'm inclined to make fun (always light heartedly, I hope!) of other people's work for plot holes, I should take the trouble to fix that in my own work. I think that goes well with being character-focused, though, as plot holes mean either violating physics, or more often, violating characters' personalities.

If you're interested in hearing about other books and essays that I write, you can follow me on Facebook (facebook.com/ChristopherTLansdown) and if you're interested in that plus the occasional joke or observation on life, Twitter (@ctlansdown). My personal website (www.chrislansdown.com) has information on all of the novels I've published. It also has current contact information for me and I love to hear from readers, so please consider stopping by.

Acknowledgements

I would like to thank Brother Owen Sadlier, OSF, who gave me the idea for a Franciscan third order regular of consulting detectives, and who also served as a test reader for me.

I'd like to thank Janette Ramos for doing such a great job on the cover art.

I'd like to thank Autumn Worth, who copy-edited the final draft and suggested some definite improvements.

I'd like to thank Harry Colin, Muna Hashim Pavlik, and Misty Woods who served as test readers of this story in its nearly final form.

I'd like to thank the creators and administrators of National Novel Writing Month, as the first draft of this story was written as a NaNoWriMo project.

MORE FROM CHRISTOPHER LANSDOWN

A STITCH IN SPACE

A priest travelling as a passenger on a deep space cargo ship has plenty of time to get to know the other passengers. And then space pirates attack.

ORDINARY SUPERHEROES

Three superheroes who foil petty crimes get dragged into a quest to save the world in this fun adventure story.

MORE FROM
SILVER EMPIRE

LOVE AT FIRST BITE

BY DECLAN FINN

Honor At Stake
Demons Are Forever
Live and Let Bite
Good to the Last Drop

THE PRODIGAL SON

BY RUSSELL NEWQUIST

War Demons
Spirit Cooking (forthcoming)

PAXTON LOCKE

BY DANIEL HUMPHREYS

Fade
Night's Black Agents
Come, Seeling Night (forthcoming)

CPSIA information can be obtained
at www.ICGtesting.com
Printed in the USA
BVHW030641230520
580188BV00002B/419